BLESSING AND CURSE

A CURSED WITCH MYSTERY

ELLE ADAMS

To be notified when Elle Adams's next book is released, sign up to her author newsletter.

When a werewolf, a vampire, and two witches walked into a building, you knew trouble was about to start. No, it wasn't the beginning of a joke—and since the building in question was full of paranormals of all sorts, it wasn't even especially unusual.

Not that the ordinary people on London's streets knew what the posh-looking office building was used for, thanks to the warding spells around its perimeter that repelled anyone who wasn't in the know about the paranormal world. Which was most people. From this side of the wards, the roar of traffic in the background was muted to a faint hum, and not so much as a smudge of dirt marred the pristine marble steps leading up to the front doors.

Only a few weeks had passed since I'd last set foot inside the Wardens' headquarters, but it felt like an age. For one thing, last time I'd had a vampire in a body bag in tow, but this time, I walked alongside a vampire who was, inexplicably, on my team.

Team. A word I still had trouble believing applied to me in any capacity. I'd never been known to play well with others

—though the same could be said of the vampire in question, who slouched at the back of the group looking like a teenager whose long-suffering parents had dragged to a museum. How Tam had convinced him to put on a suit, I had no idea, though Callum might have helped. The red-haired werewolf looked unusually serious in his own smart attire, while Farley strode beside him, her trembling hands clenched at her sides, her demure skirt and jacket making her look more like a secretary than a witch.

And then there was me. I'd dressed in my only nice outfit, a skirt and blouse that were somewhat wrinkled from sitting in the back of my wardrobe for years, and I'd already managed to scuff my polished shoes on the short walk to the building. With one hand, I tucked a strand of dark-brown hair that the wind had blown loose back into my ponytail. With the other, I pulled out my wand, ready to hand it over to the security guard on the other side of the door. No weapons were allowed in the Wardens' interrogation rooms, and I felt the absence of the usual set of knives on my belt acutely as I walked into the lobby.

Those thoughts fled when I caught sight of the team leader waiting for us. Tam's long dark hair was carefully combed, his suit impeccable, and if we weren't here for an interrogation, I might have taken a longer moment to appreciate the view. As it was, I was more concerned with the stern-faced female goblin who waited to usher us into a hallway off the side. "You must be Tam Juniper."

Tam inclined his head. "Yes, and this is my team."

Yet again, I felt a weird dissonance at the word, but when four large ogres stepped in to flank our group as we walked, I was glad not to be alone. We entered a corridor lined with doors, where one of the ogres beckoned Tam to follow him into a small office. I should have guessed we'd be sent into separate rooms and questioned separately to see if our stories added up, but my heart still sank to see Tam disappear into the room and leave the rest of us to our fates. One by one, the ogres peeled away, each taking a different team member with them until only I remained.

"This way." The ogre—female, dressed in a sharp suit designed to fit her six-foot-something broad frame—beckoned me into an office, having to duck under the doorframe to enter. I always figured the reason so many ogres worked for the Wardens was that it was nearly impossible for them to blend into regular society without relying on magic to hide their craggy green features and sharp-looking tusks.

Granted, some of us had trouble blending into regular human society for other reasons altogether. Warily, I entered and took the seat the female ogre indicated, in front of a wide desk that had also clearly been adapted to ogre size. So had the large chair that she lowered herself into, surveying me for a short moment. "You are Peregrine Jacobs, correct?"

"I—yes." I usually went by Perry, but I was under no illusions that this was a friendly chat. I didn't know this ogre, but the chances of her being a friend of my supervisor were slim, and I had a reputation among the Wardens regardless. "That's me."

"You know why you're here, Peregrine?"

"Yes." As if I could forget it. "I'm here to give a report on a mission my team was sent on recently, in which we were supposed to be assessed."

"Yes," she said. "You were to be assessed by one of our inspectors, but he…"

"… was possessed by a demon." No point in beating around the bush. "Afterwards, we were invited here to, erm, share more information."

I think. In truth, I didn't know what the Wardens wanted us to tell them. We'd already given multiple reports on the mission, in the absence of any other witnesses, but they'd insisted on dragging us here to their head office. There was little I hated more than pointless bureaucracy, but I was curious enough about where the Inspector himself had ended up that I'd resigned myself to the inconvenience.

Not that I had a choice. One did not ignore a summons from the Wardens' head office.

"Correct," she said. "Well? Can you give me a summary of the mission?"

I'd gone over the story repeatedly with Tam and the others—both the real version and the one that we'd decided to tell the Wardens—and knew it by heart, so I began by explaining how we'd arrived in the town of Herring Cove to find Inspector Peterson waiting to assess how well our team worked together. We'd scarcely been a team for a week at the time, which meant his presence had come as a surprise to all of us, but none of us could have foreseen him turning out to be possessed by a creature that would happily have seen us all dead.

I certainly didn't insinuate that the inspector had *let* the demon possess him, nor did I mention that he'd stood in our way at every turn and outright obstructed our attempts to investigate the murders we'd been sent to solve. Since the demon was gone, and the inspector himself had denied everything stubbornly after we'd evicted his unwanted hitch-hiker, the upper-ranked Wardens had been reluctant to believe our reports of his behaviour. I had little faith that today would change anything on that front.

"Our supervisor sent people to take the inspector away," I finished. "We returned to the tower to await news from the upper office."

"I see." Her pen scratched on her notepad, though I didn't know what she had to note down that wasn't already in the Wardens' reports. I could guarantee my own list of questions was infinitely longer too. For starters, where was the inspector now? Still in jail? And just who had sent him on the mission to begin with? Who had assigned him to assess us —and why?

All I knew was that Kellen, my own supervisor, hadn't decided we needed to be assessed. While I had my doubts that anyone here had known that the inspector would end up possessed by a demon, the assessment part had seemed designed to fail us, especially me. The inspector had *told* me that the Wardens had seen me as a risk factor because of the inconvenient curse that had been placed upon me as an infant, and I couldn't say for sure whether that had been the demon talking or the man himself. The Wardens might have taken me under their wing, but that had been Kellen's choice, and not everyone had agreed. Did this woman, I wondered? If not, I'd had good reason to be concerned that this questioning would end in disaster.

Then she asked the question I'd dreaded. "This is your first team, correct? Your first time being assigned to work with others?"

"Yes." I didn't need to add any details; I could guarantee that she had my entire record in front of her, which made it clear *why* I'd never been assigned to a group before. "It is."

A moment of silence followed, and more dread bloomed in my chest. *Is this the first time she's seen my record?* I could never predict how people would react upon first discovering that I was cursed, nor could I explain its parameters. All I knew was that people around me tended to get hurt and that there was no way to counteract the curse's effects.

Well. Technically, if the person who'd cursed me in the first place died, the curse might lift of its own accord, but I wouldn't know how to tell either way, so I worked under the assumption that the curse was alive and well until proven otherwise. My general luck seemed to bear that out, though my induction into Tam's team was a recent exception to the rule. Until now, perhaps.

After all, breaking apart our team was a neat way for the Wardens to resolve the thorny problem of what to do with a group of people who'd witnessed an inspector go off the rails. Since we were a group of misfits who didn't fit in anywhere, the Wardens as a whole wouldn't suffer if we disbanded.

Our team, though? Farley, an empath who'd struggled to be around people until the team had given her a voice, would suffer the most, followed by Maurice. The surly vampire wasn't my favourite person, but he and Callum were close friends, and I couldn't imagine being separated would do either of them any favours. Yet it was Tam who held us all together. If the team disbanded, I'd never find out what Tam was. I'd never get to—

"That's all," said the ogre. "You can go."

"Huh?" I frowned, disarmed. "So … what's the verdict? I mean, are we going to be punished, or…?"

"Punished?" It was her turn to frown, though her ogre tusks made that hard to tell apart from her usual expression. "No. Why would you be?"

"I… We didn't exactly follow procedures…" Meaning we'd restrained and locked up an inspector and hit him on the head. Yes, he'd been possessed at the time, but I could never tell when the Wardens' rule-following tendencies would tighten their iron grip on us.

"Actually, your team leader behaved in exactly the way I would have expected of someone in that situation."

And the rest of us? "Ah—he did. Definitely. But I thought, since we were invited here after we already submitted our reports…"

"The details bear out." She gestured to the door. "You don't *want* to be detained, do you?"

"No." I rose to my feet, my legs shaking. I hadn't realised how badly I'd wanted to be wrong. "Ah. Thank you."

I did my best not to run out of the room, and it was lucky I didn't, because Kellen was waiting outside for me. His hulking frame and curved tusks might have scared anyone who'd never met an ogre before, but I grinned at the sight of him. Kellen had been a presence in my life since he'd appointed himself my unofficial watcher when he'd discovered I was a witch—long before I'd been legally old enough to join the Wardens myself. He'd also been the first person I'd called when the last mission had broken out in chaos, and he'd suspected something was amiss with the inspector, though he hadn't been able to stop the Wardens from hauling us in for questioning.

"Hey." Then I saw he was alone. "Where are the others?"

"They're still being questioned."

"I was the first to be let out?" That couldn't be right. I was usually the *last* to escape interrogations, but I wasn't about to complain, least of all to Kellen. As my supervisor and the person with the authority to stop the Wardens from punishing me or the others for the inspector's actions, the poor guy had dealt with the brunt of the paperwork after the mission, and I'd never be able to satisfactorily repay him if I lived to be a thousand.

"That's right," he said. "We can wait outside."

I was all too happy to get out of the stuffy corridor, so I followed him out into the lobby. While I'd spent a lot of time in the Wardens' headquarters, I'd never been comfortable in any part of this building except Kellen's own office upstairs. The judging stares—both real and imaginary—were too prevalent. Not until the guard at the doors had returned my wand and we reached the steps leading out of the building did the knot in my chest loosen.

I stuck my wand up my sleeve, since my current attire

didn't have any decently sized pockets. "I can't believe I'm the first out."

"You've been in the team the least amount of time," Kellen reminded me. "The others have more questions to answer, but they'll be fine."

"What about the inspector?" I asked him in a low voice. "Is he still in jail?"

The lack of updates had bugged me, though I'd be more than happy never to set eyes on Inspector Peterson again, possessed or otherwise.

"For now, yes," Kellen said, not meeting my eyes. "However, he'll likely be freed by the month's end."

"They can't let him out," I protested. "He let himself be possessed by a demon. The two might even have worked together."

"That wasn't why he was jailed, Perry, and you know that," he said. "He broke the rules on two missions and tried to sabotage your attempt to attain justice, which wasn't a light offence, but it was light compared to teaming up with a demon. Unfortunately, there's no proof that he did anything of his own volition."

"If it's not a light offence, why's he being set free?" Did I need to ask, really? "Let me guess. He pulled some strings here."

"Perry," he said. "Please don't say that in front of anyone else."

I scowled. "Isn't it true?"

"Whether it's true or not, anyone can make an appeal for a second chance. The inspector isn't unusual in that."

"People are more likely to believe him than they are us." The inspector outranked me, and he'd done a fair number of favours for the Wardens over the years, but that didn't make him above corruption. Would anyone take the word of a cursed witch over his, though? Except for Kellen, the answer was assuredly no.

Behind us, the door opened, and Callum and Farley emerged from the building. The latter pocketed her wand, surprise crossing her face when she saw us. "They let you out first?"

"I'm shocked, too, believe me," I said. "That's three of us…"

"Tam will take the longest, being the team leader," Callum said. "I don't expect it'll be long, though, right?"

I looked to Kellen for confirmation. He nodded. "I can trust you to wait out here while I go back inside, can't I?"

"Of course," I said. "I won't get myself into trouble. Honest."

I was being truthful, too, for once. Despite my annoyance at the Wardens' leniency towards the inspector, I'd never sabotage the second chance I'd been given. When Kellen reentered the building, Maurice was next to come and join us on the steps, and I began to let myself hope that we would get out of this without my curse ruining the day.

A short time passed before Tam emerged, and my heart skipped when his green eyes scanned our group and lingered on me for an instant. "Oh, good. You're all here."

"Where else would we be?" asked Farley. "We're good to go."

"I thought…" He trailed off and then shook his head. "I thought it would be more complex than that, but I can't complain."

"So did I." And I was sure that I was the one Tam had been worried about. While I knew there was a very good reason for that that had zero to do with special treatment on my part, I couldn't help grinning all the same. "We're being sent back to the tower?"

He inclined his head. "Yes."

"Excellent." I pulled out my wand. "Ready?"

"No," growled Maurice. "Not if you're going to drop me in another puddle."

"The thought never crossed my mind." When he made a sceptical noise, I added, "I was going to leave you on the roof."

I was only teasing, but the vampire could get out of any scrape without difficulty, including being stranded on a rooftop. With an eye roll, he turned away. "I'm going to walk."

"Have fun with that." London to Northumberland was hardly a light stroll, but vampires could cross miles in the time it took to blink, and it would be easier for me to take the rest of us back without an extra passenger. "Everyone else ready?"

"You bet," said Farley.

In one wave of my wand, we vanished from the steps and left the city behind. The hum of traffic was replaced with birdsong, the skyline was substituted by a gravel path bordered by thick trees, and in place of the Wardens' head-quarters stood the castle that had become my new home. The squat building with its narrow windows and heavy wooden doors didn't look like somewhere I would have ever thought I'd consider home, but I had to resist the urge to skip up the stone steps to the front door. I let Tam walk in front and unlock the door, and I grinned so hard that my face ached.

Just inside the tower entrance lay a doorway leading into a room that formed both a gym and the team's planning room, while a stone staircase led up to the main floor, which contained the living room and kitchen. Our rooms were up on the top floor, but while Callum and Farley went straight upstairs to change out of their formal clothing, Tam lingered near the balcony overlooking the lower staircase, his expres-sion preoccupied.

"Hey…" I walked to him, wondering what his own questioning had been like. He was the team leader, so the Wardens would have undoubtedly grilled him more than the rest of us. "What's up?"

His expression smoothed out when I addressed him. "Nothing. I'm glad the upper management didn't give you any trouble."

"Did you think they would?" I asked. "I know I've had issues with them before, but our stories added up. Didn't they?"

"That's right." A furrow appeared in his brow. "It makes me wonder why they invited us all there, if not to ask anything they didn't already know."

"Pointless bureaucracy," I answered. "Kellen said the inspector was likely to be freed from confinement within the month. Did you know?"

"I guessed," he replied. "I don't think we can challenge his sentence being cut short. We don't have the authority."

My hands clenched. "I thought not. Did they say anything about whether he'd be given back his old privileges?"

"I can't imagine that'll happen right away. Likely he'll be reassigned to another department and not allowed to assess teams."

He shouldn't be allowed to work there at all. But I didn't have the power to challenge the Wardens. Even Tam didn't, and there was no telling what version of the story Inspector Peterson would give his colleagues. One that painted our team as the villains and himself as a helpless victim, no doubt.

I did my best to banish those thoughts from my mind. It wouldn't do any good to dwell on the inspector's incoming freedom, and besides, we'd won the only victory that mattered.

"What's happening next?" I asked Tam. "Were you given another mission?"

"No," he said, "but I didn't expect one. They'll take a while to process our paperwork, and I expect we'll have a reprieve until then."

"Could be worse." I was all too happy to enjoy the break and to revel in the knowledge that we were allowed to continue as a team.

Everything was back to normal … except for the inspector's freedom and the question of what would come next.

2

———

Our reprieve lasted for two days, which was longer than I'd expected. On the morning of the third day after our meeting with upper management, Tam came into the kitchen and greeted the rest of us with the news that we'd been given another mission.

"Already?" I glanced at Callum, who sat on my other side at the wooden table where we ate most of our meals, and whose surprise mirrored my own. "The head office didn't waste any time."

"No, but I expected as much." Tam took a seat at the table opposite me, with Farley on one side and Maurice on the other. "There's no sense in leaving us confined to the tower when we're more use out in the field."

I had to agree, for once. I didn't do well with sitting around twiddling my thumbs, and while the tower contained no shortage of entertainment, I needed a purpose, something to focus on that wasn't our recent questioning and the inspector's impending freedom.

"Fair enough," Callum said. "What's the mission?"

Tam reached into his coat. "I'm not entirely sure why they

called the Wardens, but it's a missing persons case in a nearby village."

"Missing persons?" I echoed. "Meaning they were taken by monsters, I assume?"

"The reports say a small child disappeared in the forest under unusual circumstances." He held up a slim folder. "This contains all the information the Wardens have, but we'll need to speak to the police when we get there."

"You already said yes?" Maurice asked, a bite to his tone. "Without asking us?"

"I didn't say yes," Tam replied. "But it's one of those cases in which the answer is assumed to be yes unless someone on the team raises an objection. Did you have one?"

Everyone looked at the vampire, who stiffened. "I didn't say I was going to object, but we don't know anything about this village or these people."

"We didn't on our last mission either." I didn't under-stand why the vampire was so disgruntled, since he'd seemed as restless as me. He'd hardly spent any time inside the tower since our return from London, which I had to admit was an improvement on him sneakily leaving spiders in my room. "The information is in the file if you want it. Right, Tam?"

Tam obligingly laid the folder down on the table, and Maurice snatched it out of the air with a vampire's typical speed. He flipped open the file, gave the contents a brief scan, and then tossed it aside with a snort. "There's nothing in there."

"Let's have a look." Callum reached for the folder. "We've been called to a village called Pleasance Grove … where a child disappeared in the woods. No evidence of foul play, but if the parents were concerned enough to call the Wardens, I assume there's more to the case than meets the eye."

"Isn't that always the way?" Farley swivelled toward our

team leader. "Tam, are we definitely the first Wardens they've called? There aren't any inspectors in the area?"

Tension rippled among the group at the memory, but Tam shook his head. "No inspectors. I asked. Also, the village is so small that they don't even have a place for visitors to stay within walking distance."

"Like Grim Crag?" said Callum, making another bout of tension rise among everyone at the table. "Except Pleasance Grove is a much nicer name."

"Appearances can be deceptive." I drummed my fingers on the wooden edge. "Not everyone with a missing persons case calls the Wardens. If they did, we'd never have any peace."

"I wouldn't say we're likely to have a repeat of the inspector incident," Callum said. "What're the odds of it happening twice?"

"Don't tempt fate," Farley scolded him in a good-natured fashion. "Let's see that folder."

I watched her open the folder, mostly to avoid making eye contact with Maurice. *Don't tempt fate ...* or rather, don't tempt the bad-luck curse. The vampire had been the first to find out and expose that I was cursed with a lifetime of bad luck, though it had turned out Tam had been aware all along and had accepted me into the team regardless. So had the others—though Maurice had been reluctant, and I'd always wondered if he, like me, was always waiting for the other shoe to drop. That we'd managed to get through the questioning unscathed was one point in my favour, but his current attitude suggested he was spoiling for a fight. Not that the vampire was the pinnacle of friendliness at the best of times.

Farley flipped to the end of the file. "Sounds pretty straightforward. I don't have any objections."

"Neither do I," Callum added.

"I doubt I will either." I took the folder next, but I didn't need to read the notes to know that we were taking this case. According to the file, the missing child was a seven-year-old girl called Joy Hutchins, but otherwise the notes said nothing the others didn't already know. Putting the folder aside, I raised a brow at Maurice. "Well? That's all of us who've said yes except for one."

The vampire glowered. "You said there wasn't anywhere to stay nearby, Tam. I'm not staying in another mouldy hostel."

"You really hated Herring Cove that much?" Callum referred to the unpleasant village in which we'd spent our last mission. Not only would I forever associate the place with our battle with demons, but days had passed, and I had yet to get the smell of fish out of my clothing. "Tam, is this Pleasance Grove place close to the tower?"

"Actually, yes," said Tam. "It's close enough that we should easily be able to get back and forth from the tower if this turns out to take longer than a day. You won't have a problem with that, Maurice."

"Fine." The vampire shot me a dirty look that made me suspect his objection had pertained mostly to the idea of having to rely on me to transport everyone to the site of the mission. Okay, I may have dropped him in a puddle or two while using transportation spells to ferry the team around, but that had been an accident. Well. The first time had, anyway.

"We'll set out later this morning," Tam said. "Say, eleven. Sound good?"

"Sure." With the vampire's objection taken care of, I returned to drinking my morning coffee. "It'll be nice to take on a case a bit closer to the tower."

"But not *too* close," added Farley. "We've had too much experience with creepy forests around here."

"True." Our first case as a team had taken place in the woodland directly in front of the castle's front doors and had involved a possessed *tree,* of all things. It'd be a while before I could look at a forest and not imagine the trees moving of their own accord, but I had a hard time believing the Wardens had assigned us to three demon-related cases in a row.

In any case, this one seemed more straightforward than our previous missions, and I wouldn't object to having more time here in the cosy tower that had, inexplicably, become my new home.

An hour passed, during which we finished breakfast, cleaned up the tower, and otherwise prepared for the mission. I was already dressed in my usual jeans and T-shirt, but I grabbed my coat on the way out. It was early August, but the weather up north was temperamental, and the cold breeze off the coast made it feel more like autumn than summer. I also packed a rucksack with weapons—not enough to go overboard but enough that I could deal with any paranormal monster we might run into.

At eleven, we gathered on the gravel path outside, next to the bright-red sports car that Maurice never let anyone else take a ride in. When the vampire sauntered out of the tower, I called to him, "Hey, Maurice. How about we take your car instead of walking?"

He called me a rude, uncalled-for name. "Like I'd let you wreck my car."

"Maurice," said Callum. "She has a point. If the village is within driving distance—"

"I'm not driving my car to the middle of a forest when there's likely a monster loose in the area," he said flatly.

"Nobody said anything about a monster," said Farley.

Maurice scoffed. "Why else would we have been called in?"

Fair point. If I'd had a car that fancy, I might not have been keen to see it damaged either. "Just an idea. Transportation charm it is. Everyone ready?"

"Of course," said Callum.

Farley and Tam nodded, but the vampire strode away. "I'll race you there."

"Hey—wait." I scowled when he took off at a fast stride. "That's cheating. I don't even know what our destination looks like yet."

"Here." Tam held up his phone and showed a photograph of a cluster of houses in a wooded area, and I did my best to commit it to memory. Transportation spells were risky if one hadn't been to a place before, but it was the fastest way to get there without having to piggyback on Maurice.

I pictured the area in my mind's eye and waved my wand, and a flash of light engulfed the world. An instant later, my feet sank into mud, and a sharp branch thwacked me on the forehead. Eyes watering, I looked up to see the others had fared slightly better—except for Farley, who was up to her shoulders in a giant bush of brambles.

"Sorry!" I sidestepped the branch, rubbing my forehead, while Callum moved to rescue Farley from the brambles. "Tam? You here?"

I couldn't see our team leader at all, but my moment of panic went away when he stepped into view out of a clearing behind us. He looked momentarily disconcerted, though his expression cleared when he saw us. "Everyone okay?"

"Just about," said Farley, shaking another bramble off her sleeve. "Where are we?"

"In the right place, I hope." I couldn't see anyone else around aside from the four of us, but the small village ought to be nearby, hidden among the trees.

"I think we are," Tam said. "The forest looks similar to the one in the photos."

"Anyone got a map?" Farley pulled out her phone. "No … no internet signal in here."

"I didn't expect one." Tam took the lead, returning to the clearing in which he'd landed. The rest of us followed, mostly so that we'd have room to talk without walking into any more branches.

Callum sniffed the air. "I can't smell anyone, but if we're close, I should be able to pick up the scent of habitation when the wind shifts."

"Good," said Tam. Was it just me, or did he sound more on edge than usual? "I think that's our best bet."

"I wish Maurice was here to see that I didn't do this on purpose," I muttered, picking leaves out of my hair. "Do you think *he* reached the right place?"

"No clue." Callum tripped over a giant tree root and caught his balance on another. "I'd be surprised if even he didn't get lost in here."

The forest was so dense that a village could have been hidden anywhere amid the thick oak trees, and I wouldn't have known. Clusters of bright toadstools sprouted between thick roots and patches of brambles, and the forest overall had the air of somewhere that had been untouched by humans for a while and intended to stay that way.

"I guess we can look for any signs of the monster while we walk to the village," I remarked to the others, wondering if we were anywhere near where the missing child had disappeared.

"Don't say that." Farley shuddered. "I bet she just wandered off the path. A monster doesn't need to be involved for someone to get lost in here."

"Agreed." Callum ambled along, occasionally swearing when his head collided with a low-hanging branch. "I don't see anything dodgy."

Tam, who was the same height as the werewolf, somehow

avoided crashing into anything while he led the way. He was more used to this kind of setting, I assumed, though I didn't know for sure. I knew next to nothing about his history, in fact, and he'd been almost as tight lipped about his past as I had when I'd initially moved to the tower. I didn't know which part of the UK he came from or, to be honest, even what type of paranormal he was. The question was not generally polite to ask, and my experience usually made it easy to tell with a single glance. In any case, he seemed at home in the forest, despite the worry surrounding him like a cloak. I didn't blame him, frankly. This wasn't the creepiest forest I'd been in—that honour went to the one with the possessed tree, which I was still reluctant to go back into—but the memory was all too fresh in my mind.

Lost in thought, I also tripped over a tree branch, catching my balance in time to avoid face-planting. "Nature strikes again."

Callum sniffed the air, once, twice, and his expression brightened. "I smell smoke. This way."

"Smoke means civilisation," Farley said. "Or a forest fire."

"I'm going with the former." I stepped around yet another cluster of poisonous-looking toadstools and sniffed the air, but all I could smell were earth and damp leaves.

"Gotcha." Callum bounded ahead in triumph, toward an area where the trees had thinned out enough to see the outlines of several stone houses. Smoke billowed out from brick chimneys, and nearby, Maurice leaned against a tree, a bored expression on his face.

"There you are," he said. "I thought I'd be here all day."

"We're fine." Tam sounded as relieved to get out of the forest as the rest of us did, which was unusual for him.

Maurice's attention went straight to me. "Looks like I won the race."

"Too bad I didn't bring a medal."

He smirked. "What did you do, get into a punch-up with a local already?"

"No." I lifted my hand to my forehead. The branch I'd hit must have left a bruise. "This forest isn't friendly."

"You didn't have to try that hard to prove you were crap at transportation spells."

"Why would I crash into a tree on purpose?" I lowered my hand. "It's not always about you. Transportation spells are unpredictable on a good day."

He should know, since he'd been a wizard when he'd been alive, which surely hadn't been that long ago. He was young by vampire standards and acted like a sulky teenager at the best of times, which made it difficult to tell his actual age, but unlike with Tam, I had no curiosity whatsoever about his history.

Maurice ignored my comment. "I've already had time to circle the whole village and look around. It's almost as tiny as Hexworth is."

"And?" Tam asked. "Did you see anything that struck you as suspicious?"

"No." He shrugged. "Should I have?"

"We're here for a reason," I reminded him. "Though we didn't see any signs of foul play in the forest, did we?"

"No ... there was no sign of the missing girl." Something in Tam's manner suggested he didn't quite agree with my assessment. Maybe I was imagining things, but Farley had gone tense as well, and she was the best of us all at picking up on unspoken emotions.

"There can't be more than a hundred people here," Maurice declared. "You'd think someone would have spotted a kid who wandered off."

"The forest is a maze," I pointed out.

"Obviously, I have a better sense of direction than you,"

he said. "I could have taken a nap on the way and still have beaten you."

"No need to rub it in," I said. "We had time to look around the woods while you were here, and I didn't see any typical monster signs. Did anyone else?"

"There's no such thing as a typical monster sign," said Callum. "Besides, it might be a normal human-related kidnapping. We'll have to talk to the person who called the Wardens first. Do we know who that was?"

"Yes… I have the name and address." Tam pulled out his phone. "Mrs Clementine Hutchins … the mother of the missing girl, I'm guessing."

"She called the Wardens?" I asked. "Not the police?"

"I'm guessing she started with the police." He lowered his phone. "She might not be at home, so we'll go to the local police station first."

Hmm. Had she called us out of desperation because the police had failed to find her missing daughter? Or did she have another reason—such as a need for the Wardens' specialised skills?

3

I didn't have much time to puzzle over why we'd been invited here, because as soon as we entered the village proper, we drew immediate attention from the locals. The few people on the street whispered and pointed at us, especially Tam. From what I could tell, this community mostly consisted of witches, wizards, and maybe a few shifters. No vampires, though the people didn't pay much attention to Maurice, who slouched at the back. Instead, it was Tam who caught their attention. When he asked a young woman for directions, I thought she was going to faint.

"It's … that way," she said huskily, eyeing him with apparent awe.

What's with her? Sure, Tam was good looking, but I didn't fall over every time he walked into a room. Maybe they'd just never seen a stranger before. I shook off the irrational surge of irritation and followed the others down the street.

The police station, if you could call it that, was a house that was only marginally bigger than the other dwellings. When Tam knocked on the door, a surprisingly young-looking man with a weedy face and a goatee answered.

"Oh, hello." He looked us over with mild surprise. "Are you … the Wardens?"

"Yes, we are," Tam said. "I assume you know why we're here?"

"Yes … you'd better come in."

He beckoned to us to enter a small office, though again, the word 'office' was a stretch, since it didn't even have a desk. The guy—Glenn, he turned out to be called—sat down on a sofa with his laptop balanced on his knees while the rest of us crowded into the room around the edges.

"Can you tell us more about what happened?" asked Tam. "Our reports didn't contain much information on Joy Hutchins's disappearance. Did her mother come to the police immediately and report her daughter was missing?"

"Yes … yes, she did." He put his laptop aside, a thoughtful expression on his face. "She said her child disappeared in the woods near her house. I sent people to look, but they couldn't find her. That was, ah, two days ago."

Hmm. "How thoroughly did they search the woods? I mean, it's kind of a maze in there."

He blinked at me. "Most of us are familiar with the forest. I can assure you we searched the best we could."

"Why would she have decided to call the Wardens?" asked Tam. "Did she think our specialist skills would be needed?"

He frowned, his goatee drooping. "Don't the Wardens help in cases like this?"

Actually, we hunt monsters most of the time. I refrained from saying that, but I had to wonder if this guy knew anything about the Wardens at all.

"Sometimes, depending on whether we're needed," Tam said, presumably thinking along the same lines. "Ah, is it possible for us to talk to the missing child's mother?"

"Of course," he said. "She was the one who called you, right? I'm surprised she was able to get through. We don't have much of a reliable phone signal out here in the woods."

That figured. I didn't think we'd get much more useful information out of the police, and we were better off talking to the person who'd wanted us to come here, especially if Mrs Hutchins had intended to bypass the authorities for a reason.

I gladly left the crowded room and assessed our location. Pleasance Grove appeared to consist of three main roads and a handful of short cul-de-sacs branching off, which made it look deceptively easy to find the right house. At least until we realised there weren't any street signs. It didn't help that virtually everyone we passed in the street stopped to stare at us, or whisper, or both.

"This place doesn't get outsiders much, I assume," I muttered to my teammates as we walked.

"I'm getting that impression myself," said Callum. "Farley, are you okay?"

All eyes turned to her—as the empath, she was more attuned to others' emotions than the rest of us—but she nodded. "They aren't hostile. They're just … wary. And curious. I think you're right."

Maurice scoffed. "Of course they don't get many visitors. They're a tiny paranormal community who don't even have a proper coven."

"How do you know that?" I asked. "You haven't been reading people's minds, have you?"

"Of course not," he said. "They were talking. If you were paying attention, you'd know too."

"All right." I held up my hands. "No need to be prickly. We don't need to make enemies in a village as small as this one."

"Agreed." Tam halted at a fork in the road. "This way."

If you asked me, we could have found the right house in less time just by knocking on each door until we got the right one. Tam was right, though, and we found Mr and Mrs Hutchinses' house in the shadow of a large maple tree.

When he knocked, the door creaked inward, revealing a pale witch with wild, curly dark hair and a pair of glasses that magnified her watery eyes. Swaying on the spot, the witch took one look at me and screamed.

"What—?" I took a step back, startled.

The witch staggered back and clutched her forehead, shrieking again. At my side, Farley gasped, and Callum caught her in his arms before she collapsed.

"This is going well," Maurice said helpfully.

Tam came to the rescue, approaching the cowering witch. "Excuse me? We're not here to harm you. We're here to help. You called the Wardens, didn't you?"

The witch whimpered, pointing over at me. "She's … she's…"

Tam strode into the doorway and caught her arm before she could fall, and as I watched, he expertly steered her through the open door to a living room. Callum, supporting a shaking Farley in his arms, peered through the window. "What's with her?"

"She's terrified." Farley lifted her head, clutching Callum's arm for balance. "I don't know why."

"Because of her." Maurice indicated me. "Obviously."

Heat rushed to my face, but I was too bewildered to be mad at him. Through the open curtains, I glimpsed Tam conversing with the witch inside the living room—and noticed a crystal ball sitting on the mantelpiece. Then the penny dropped.

"I think she's all right now," Callum observed. "I don't know what that was about."

I do. The witch was a Seer, and this was far from the first time I'd elicited that reaction from someone with the ability to see the future. How could I have forgotten so easily?

Maurice snorted. "We're drawing too much attention. I'm going for a walk."

"Don't get lost in the forest." If he'd been anyone else, I'd have wondered if he was trying to give me some privacy to explain what was going on to the others. Despite her fear, Farley looked utterly confused, and so did Callum.

"Tam's calmed her down," he observed, squinting through the window. "Hey—that's a crystal ball in there."

"Exactly. She's a Seer." It said volumes about how recent events had caused me to let down my guard, because for a long time, I'd been accustomed to everyone with a hint of Seeing ability reacting as that witch did when they first saw me. "Hence the screaming."

The werewolf eyed me, puzzled. "Why would a Seer be afraid of you?"

"I'm cursed, remember?" I kept my voice low. "Seers tend to be tuned into energies that regular people can't sense. I don't really know how it works, but this isn't the first time I've had a Seer nearly pass out on me."

"Poor thing," said Farley. "I felt her fear. It was genuine."

I made a noncommittal noise and returned my attention to the window, but I couldn't hear what Tam was saying to Mrs Hutchins. The last thing I needed to do was cause her to panic even more by walking into her house, but I had to wonder why her Seeing ability hadn't warned her I was coming.

"Oh—was this why you didn't want to join a team when you came to the tower?" asked Callum. "I remember you mentioned Seers had a hard time with you…"

"Pretty much," I said. "I did try to explain, but it's hard to make up for the actual experience of watching someone react like I just prophesied their own doom."

I usually had some level of sympathy, but it was tiresome to always find that people felt sorrier for the Seer than for me, the actual person with a curse on her. I didn't want to take the focus away from the matter at hand—namely, finding the missing child—but how could I possibly help with that if she couldn't look directly at me without screaming her head off?

"Is she likely to have the same reaction every single time?" Farley asked uncertainly.

"Depends on what Tam told her." As if he'd heard me, he caught my eye through the window and beckoned to the others.

Callum made for the door. "I think he wants us to come in."

"Not the best idea." Mrs Hutchins was focusing on Tam instead of the window, but that didn't mean I needed to cause her any more distress.

As Callum pushed the door inward and entered, Farley on his heels, Tam called out, "Come on in, all of you."

When I didn't budge, Tam appeared in the doorway. "Perry? You can come in."

"Are you sure?" I asked dubiously. "I don't want to cause trouble."

"It's fine." He beckoned again, and I reluctantly tailed him into the house.

As before, the witch's eyes widened at the sight of me, but she didn't scream this time. "You're the other Wardens? I didn't know they were sending a team."

"As I said, we're here to help you," Tam said. "Is it all right if the others come in?"

"Yes … yes." She cast a wary glance in my direction as she shuffled back into the living room. "I suppose. Try not to touch the crystal ball, won't you?"

I followed the others into the living room and took the last available armchair, which unfortunately happened to be right next to the crystal ball. The surface was as murky as a storm-tossed sky, and I fixed my attention on the opposite wall to avoid staring directly into the glass.

The witch leaned forward in her seat. "I'm glad they sent someone so quickly."

"We came here as soon as we could," Tam told her. "Your daughter disappeared two days ago in the forest. Is that right? Can you tell me why exactly you contacted the Wardens rather than the police?"

"I..." She trailed off, staring into the distance. "I had a vision. I couldn't completely make sense of it, but it was clear that I needed expertise."

A shiver ran down my spine. Perhaps she hadn't called the Wardens because of a worried parental overreaction but because her Seer abilities had convinced her that she'd need our help. On the other hand, it would help if she'd been clear about *what* she'd seen that had convinced her to call the Wardens. Seers weren't known for specificity. Or accuracy.

"What did you see?" I figured we might as well get to the point. "We work better with as many details as possible."

She shuddered, wringing her hands. "I saw her. My daughter. She was in the forest."

"And?" I pressed. "Whereabouts? And was there anyone else in there?"

"It was very bright," she said. "Too bright for me to see..."

"Like a spell?" asked Callum.

"I don't know," she murmured. "I don't know, but I was sure I heard ... laughing."

"Whose laughing?"

"I think ... I think it was my Joy."

"You heard your daughter laughing?" Seers' visions weren't bound to a time or place, so it was entirely possible she'd seen an utterly harmless vision several years or more into the future. "Is that why you called us? Or was there something else?"

If someone had kidnapped her child, they could certainly have used magic to do so, but that was no reason to call in the experts. We only got involved if a magical monster needed hunting, but if I said that, I might well send her into hysterics again.

"No … I didn't see anything else," she said. "I just had … had a bad feeling."

"What kind of bad feeling?" Would it kill her to be a tiny bit more specific? "Like … like she was in danger?"

The remaining colour drained from her face. "Yes … yes. I'm sure Joy is in danger. Please … help me find her."

"We'll do our best," said Tam. "Is there anything else you can tell us? Where did you last see her?"

"In … in the back garden." She pointed over her shoulder with her trembling hand. "She was playing, and…"

"And?" Tam prompted.

"I turned my back for a minute, and when I looked for her, she was gone." She sniffed loudly. "We live right next to the woods, so I'm guessing she climbed over the fence, but I don't know where she is."

That didn't rule out a human kidnapper, but she hadn't given us much to work with either. Unfortunately, Seers usually only knew the meanings of their visions in hindsight, if at all, which amounted to guesswork in my book.

I figured we'd already outstayed our welcome, and I got to my feet first. The movement unintentionally drew her gaze to the crystal ball, and a stifled gasp escaped her. "It's happening again!"

"Huh?" I dropped my gaze to the swirling greyness, none the wiser about what she was looking at. Its surface was impenetrable to my non-Seer's eyes. "Can you see anything?"

"You aren't in there." She lifted her head, her gaze snapping up to a startled Tam. "You aren't in there either."

"It's okay." Tam used a reassuring tone. "Will you be all right? Do you want me to call someone?"

She shook her head. "No … my husband will be home from work soon."

"All right." Tam led the way out of the room, and the rest of us muttered awkward goodbyes before following him. Outside, he scanned the area with a faint hint of worry. "Where's Maurice?"

"He got bored and went for a walk," I said. "I assume he can't have gone far."

"I'd rather not split up if we can help it," Tam said. "While we're here, we ought to have a look around the scene where the girl disappeared."

"Assuming Mrs Hutchins was right," said Callum. "She didn't seem very sure of herself, did she?"

"Seers rarely are," I said. "They see the future in confusing flashes that don't make much sense even to themselves, let alone anyone else. I'm not convinced she saw anything that would justify calling the Wardens."

"She might have," said Farley. "Seers might not be sure of their senses, but their intuition is usually spot on."

Tam looked at me, and I ducked my head. While he was well aware of my curse's effect on Seers, it was more embarrassing that Tam had witnessed her reaction than the rest of the team, somehow. "We'll see."

Tam motioned towards the woods at the end of the street. "We can get in the forest that way and loop around the back of the house. Ideally, Maurice is waiting in there."

"He doesn't have many other places to go," I said. "Not if he wants to avoid being gawked at."

As Tam took the lead, Callum glanced sideways at me. "Did she really say she couldn't see you in the crystal ball? Is that normal?"

"Pretty sure she said she couldn't see any of us," I

muttered. "Vampires don't show up in crystal balls, so maybe Maurice being with us clouded her vision." I hoped that was it, not that my curse had further obscured an already confusing case.

"I forgot that about vampires," said Callum. "Hope that doesn't make it harder for us to find her kid."

"I don't think any of us were in the vision of the forest she described," Farley said. "Though she wasn't clear on whether anyone else was there either. Unless... What did she see when she looked at you? Was her kid there?"

"I doubt it," I replied. "I've never got a clear explanation of what Seers actually see when they look at me, but I can guarantee she saw nothing that had to do with her missing child. She'd have had the same reaction on a regular day."

Or so I hoped. With general bad-luck curses like mine, there was no way to disentangle cause and effect to work out what had been the result of the curse and what was due to outside forces. It wouldn't make this case any less tricky to resolve, that was for sure.

"All right." Callum put on a determined stride as we entered the forest. "We assume the girl went for a wander through the back of the garden somewhere in here..."

He trailed off, seeing that Tam had come to a sudden halt. Our team leader's gaze was fixed on the clearing ahead, and my heart sank when I saw two figures facing one another like a pair of combatants before a fight.

Maurice stood eye to eye with a man I didn't recognise, the vampire's fangs out and his posture promising violence.

4

"Maurice," Tam called to the vampire. "What are you doing?"

Both the vampire and the stranger swivelled towards us but maintained their defensive stances. I had an inkling that if we hadn't shown up when we did, they'd have been at each other's throats, and while vampires could literally run circles around regular people, the stranger hadn't backed off when he saw Maurice's fangs.

"What are you doing?" Callum strode over to join the vampire, eyeing the stranger with a frown. "Sorry about our friend."

The guy scowled straight back at him. "Your friend could do with learning some manners before he gets himself staked."

Ordinarily, I'd have agreed with the 'manners' part, but the word 'staked' rang alarm bells in my head. The guy didn't look like a local either. He was dressed like a hiker, in practical clothing and thick boots, and had several weapons strapped to his belt. In fact, a stake might have been among them. A jolt of familiarity hit me. I knew what he was … a paranormal hunter.

Tam stepped in. "Our team was sent in to assist with finding a missing local girl. We're working with the police. Might I ask why you're here?"

His tone was polite, but frost clung to each word. I guessed he'd come to the same conclusion that I had. *Who called the paranormal hunters here?*

The man's jaw tensed. "I was called here to find a missing kid too. I got here yesterday."

"Doesn't look like you've got very far," said Maurice.

"How would *you* know, vampire?"

"Unless you're hiding the missing kid in that backpack of yours, you haven't found her." He gestured towards the large pack at the hunter's feet. What did he have in there, more stakes?

"Who called you?" I asked. "Not Mrs Hutchins. She called *us.* Unless we were called in because you failed at your job?"

A flush darkened the hunter's face. "The police called me, actually, and there's no need for any of you to be here as well."

"Why exactly were you standing in here arguing with Maurice instead of looking for Joy, then?" I queried.

"The vampire ambushed me," the hunter snarled. "I was obliged to defend myself."

"A likely story." I never thought I'd take the vampire's side, but all the paranormal hunters I'd met so far had been unpleasant to be around. People who signed up to get paid for hunting down shifters and vampires who broke the rules tended not to be the sort who wanted to hang out with a cursed witch like me.

"Wait a moment," Callum said. "There's no need to be so hostile with one another. We're on the same side, aren't we?"

"We have the same objective," Tam agreed, "which is why

I'd like to know who you are and why you came here. I'm Tam Juniper, leader of this team. You?"

The hunter's gaze darted over us. "The name's Dylan Crofton, and I don't need your help."

"That's nice," I said. "Since when did the hunters send people to search for missing children?"

"Hunters?" Callum asked sharply; he evidently hadn't guessed the man's occupation—and from her startled expression, neither had Farley.

"Since when did the Wardens send people to search for missing children?" Dylan retaliated.

I think there's more going on than that. I cast a glance around the forest clearing, but if there were any signs pointing at the girl's location, the hunter had probably trampled all over them. "The missing girl's mother called us. If you have an issue, feel free to take it up with the Wardens' upper management."

Callum cleared his throat. "Look, we *do* have the same purpose. We're here to find Joy and return her home. Can we focus on that?"

"There is no 'we.'" The hunter glowered at us, his arms folded across his chest. "And your management isn't here."

"We aren't going to get anywhere with that guy," I whispered to the others. "I say we do this ourselves."

"Agreed," Farley muttered back. "Tam?"

I swivelled towards him. Tam's eyes were narrowed, fixed on the hunter. "If you don't mind, we'll carry on with our mission."

"Mission." He scoffed. "Go on, get out of here."

"What do you mean, go on?" Tam's tone was as cold as the Arctic Ocean. "We aren't leaving."

"You're causing a disturbance. There are too many people in here."

"Then *you* can leave." I waved a hand, wishing the police

had *told* us he'd invited a member of one of the most unpleasant organisations in the magical world to help find Joy. No, the Wardens weren't perfect, but our excess of paperwork was a stark contrast to the way the hunters tended to shoot first and ask questions later. Literally, in some cases.

"I was here first," said Dylan. "I bet you don't know the first thing about this place. I do."

I had my doubts. Paranormal hunters were ignorant at a baseline. They didn't even have to be paranormal to join—a fair portion of them were either born into it or otherwise recruited from communities that lived in close enough proximity to paranormals that they wouldn't break the laws if they were brought into our world. I didn't judge them for not being paranormals, though. Rather, I judged them for having the patience of a rampaging manticore and less of the appeal.

"Regardless, Joy's family called us," Tam said. "This is the place where she was last seen, and her family gave us permission to look around."

He beckoned, and we followed him to the far side of the clearing, which was unfortunately still within hearing distance of the hunter. There was nowhere to go to avoid him, but I did my best to ignore the hunter's presence as Tam addressed our group.

"I know this isn't ideal," he said, "but we need to proceed as if this is a typical mission. Perry, Farley, you can look for traces of magic use in the area. Callum, can you try to pick up Joy's scent?"

"I can try," he said doubtfully. "I can't smell anyone aside from our group—and that guy, of course."

"I thought so," he said. "How about you circle back to the Hutchinses' house and see if you can pick up the scent from there? Maurice, you go with him."

"Why?" said the vampire. "I don't see why I should have to leave while that hunter guy sticks around. What if he tries to stab you in the back?"

"I'll keep an eye on him myself," Tam said. "If I need you to follow him, I'll let you know. And … if I think it's necessary for you to peer into his thoughts, I'll let you know that too."

Whoa. Even the vampire looked surprised. Tam rarely let Maurice indulge his vampiric ability to invade others' privacy. He must think the hunter was untrustworthy, which was fair enough, but I had to wonder if his own experiences with the paranormal hunters were as revealing as mine.

Asking him more questions would have to wait until Dylan was out of earshot, but the hunter remained in the background while Farley and I began our search. Farley's discomfort was obvious from the way she kept fidgeting, her gaze darting towards our unwanted companion.

"I wish he'd stop staring at us," she muttered to me. "It's creepy. Seen anything?"

"No." The tangled tree branches and thick undergrowth might have hidden more clues, but Dylan's stare followed me, making it difficult to focus on searching for signs of magical kidnappers. Or monsters. "Mrs Hutchins described a bright light in her vision, but that could describe pretty much any spell."

"Or it might have nothing to do with her missing child," she said. "Seers' visions aren't that specific, and she didn't seem sure of herself at all."

"True." I glanced up at the hunter on the opposite side of the clearing, but he didn't appear to have heard us. Did he know Mrs Hutchins was a Seer? It didn't necessarily matter if he did, but the question of why the police had neglected to mention they'd already called someone to search lingered at the back of my mind.

After a short pause, Farley whispered, "I wish he'd go away. He's not even searching for the girl."

"Have you met any paranormal hunters before? They're all like that."

"Yeah, I guess." She bit her lower lip. "When they find out my abilities, they think I'm a freak."

"You and me both." I'd thought Mrs Hutchins passing out at the sight of me was bad enough. "This is going to be a nuisance. We'll never get anywhere if he keeps getting underfoot."

We continued to search the clearing for any clues about Joy's disappearance that were invisible to the hunter's eyes. Hunters sometimes had a knack for sensing magic. I couldn't tell if that was true of our unwanted companion, but I didn't trust him to share his insights with us regardless.

By the time we'd finished searching the immediate area, Callum had reentered the clearing with a scowling Maurice at his side.

"Did you manage to pick up her scent?" I asked the former.

"I did, but I can't find it in the forest," he said. "Maybe the rain washed it away."

"It's been raining?" I didn't see much in the way of raindrops or puddles. Even the soil didn't look particularly wet, though in fairness, the tree cover was thick enough to form a shield overhead.

A scoff drew my attention to the hunter. He hadn't moved an inch since our arrival, though Tam hadn't budged from his position a few feet away either.

"What's the problem?" I asked the hunter. "Aren't you going to look around? Or did you want to wait for us to do all the work?"

"I'm here to stop you from stirring up trouble," he said. "You clearly don't have a clue what you're doing."

"Says the guy who hasn't done anything except glare at us since we got here." I turned my attention back to Tam. "What now?"

Tam indicated the backs of the nearby houses. "We'll have another chat with the police."

Good idea. Glenn had some explaining to do, though he might have neglected to mention that we weren't the only monster hunters in town out of the naive assumption that we were on the same side. He seemed to know little about the Wardens, and I doubted he was an expert on the hunters either.

I was all too happy to turn my back on Dylan, but when we left the forest, I noticed Maurice had disappeared again.

"Ah—he's not going to harass Dylan, is he?" I asked Tam in a low voice. "Don't get me wrong—he's asking for it—but we'll get kicked out of town if Maurice starts a fight."

Tam slowed his pace. "Callum, can you keep an eye out for Maurice? See if you can pick up Joy's scent in the woods too."

"All right," said Callum. The laid-back werewolf was the best choice to mediate any arguments involving the prickly vampire, but I wished Maurice would do what he was told for once.

"I hope he keeps those stakes hidden," I said as we walked past Mr and Mrs Hutchinses' house. "That Dylan guy is nothing but trouble."

"Agreed," said Farley. "He really didn't want us there."

"The feeling's mutual." I glanced through the window to the Hutchinses' house, but I didn't see anyone in the living room. "What I'd like to know is why Glenn called him and didn't tell us. Did Mrs Hutchins know, I wonder?"

"Good question." Tam led the way down the street to the fork in the road. "I'm guessing she did, but the people of this village don't strike me as necessarily familiar with how the Wardens operate. Or the hunters."

"Including the police." I lowered my voice when we reached one of the main streets, where the whispers and stares sprang up once more.

Seemingly oblivious to the attention, Tam strode towards the police station and knocked on the door.

Glenn answered him with the same expression of mild surprise he'd worn earlier. "You again? Did you already find something?"

"We searched the forest and talked to Mrs Hutchins," Tam said. "However, we ran into an unexpected individual called Dylan Crofton. I believe you invited him here yourself. You didn't mention that to us earlier."

He blinked at us. "I told you I sent people to look around the woods…"

"I thought they were other officers," I said, though there didn't appear to *be* any other officers in town. "Or locals."

"Why didn't you tell us you called the paranormal hunters?" asked Tam. "If we'd known, we'd have used a different approach."

"Why?" Glenn sounded genuinely puzzled. "The more the merrier, right?"

I suppressed a snort. He was seriously deluding himself if he thought we had any intention of working with Dylan, but evidently, he didn't know anything about the enmity between the Wardens and the hunters.

"I assumed the scene of Joy's disappearance was untouched," Tam clarified. "As it was, my team members were unable to find any clues or pick up Joy's scent."

"Scent?"

"Yes, shifters can track people by smell." Did this guy know nothing about—well, anything? "The trail ended at the forest."

Someone coughed behind us. I glanced over my shoulder and saw that Dylan had followed us up to the police station. "What are you doing here?"

"What else?" He lifted his chin. "I'm working with the police myself, since they called *me* here and not you."

"You don't have anything to report, do you?" I asked. "You weren't even looking for the missing girl."

"You don't know anything at all." He strode past our group, towards Glenn, who wore an apprehensive expression. "Officer, these so-called Wardens have been disrupting and disrespecting me. I want them out of town."

"Have they?" Glenn's gaze darted between him and Tam, and Glenn swallowed. "Aren't you all looking for the same child?"

"We told him that," I interjected. "He wouldn't listen, and he kept trying to obstruct us."

"Their vampire friend was rude to me without reason," said Dylan. "Besides, I can't do my job with a bunch of loud paranormals rampaging around the forest."

"Mrs Hutchins herself called us," I said, mostly for Glenn's benefit. "I'd say it should be her choice, don't you?"

Glenn shrank back. "Regardless of who called whom, we're all here now, aren't we? Can't you try to get along?"

Definitely not. I didn't need to speak the words aloud for Glenn to guess my response—and the hunter too—but Tam spoke up first. "My teammates and I are willing to cooperate … provided Dylan agrees to do the same."

"A likely story," he said. "You don't know anything about this village or the people here. You didn't even ask if the Hutchins family suspected anyone in particular in their daughter's disappearance or if they think a specific individual took the girl, did you?"

Well … no. But that was because she was telling us about her vision. "Did *you* talk to Mrs Hutchins? If so, she couldn't have had much faith in you to find her daughter," I said.

"That means no." A smirk flitted across Dylan's face. "If I were you, I'd look into any suspicious newcomers who moved to town recently and who were seen near the Hutchinses' house the day she vanished."

"What?" I took a step after him, but he was already walking away. "Was he serious?"

Glenn shuffled his feet. "I hoped he'd be more welcoming. You have the same goal, you know."

"Yes, we do, but he doesn't seem inclined to play well with others." My hands curled into fists as I watched the hunter walk out of sight. "What was the point in him following us here?"

To taunt us, I assumed … but was there any truth in his words? Might one of the locals know more than the police did? Given Glenn's general cluelessness, the assumption wasn't unreasonable to make.

"Never mind him," Tam said. "Glenn, I'd appreciate it if you let me know if you have any suspicions concerning Joy's disappearance. Have any of the townspeople been behaving oddly?"

"What was that about suspicious newcomers?" I jumped straight to the point. "That was way too specific for him to have made up."

Glenn withdrew into the doorway. "I assume he meant Sylvan, but I already spoke to him, and he said he didn't have anything to do with what happened to Joy."

Hmm? Was this a link worth pursuing? I didn't want to take Dylan's bait, but if this Sylvan person had been near the Hutchinses' house the day their daughter had disappeared, that made him a witness. We had no other suspects, and Dylan had been here longer than we had. What if he'd uncovered information in the past day that, for whatever reason, hadn't made it into the file we'd been given?

And who was more reliable ... the police or one of the paranormal hunters?

5

We left the police station, quietly debating among ourselves over whether to talk to the newcomer or not. While Tam thought it was worth speaking to any possible lead, I was less inclined to take the hunter's bait until the value of doing so was proven, and Farley was on the fence. When we found Callum and Maurice waiting at the edge of one of the entrances to the woods, Tam wasted no time in trying to convince them to break the tie.

"If that Dylan suspects this newcomer, I can almost guarantee they're innocent," Callum commented. "He's trying to bait us."

"That was what I said." I looked to Maurice next, hoping that our newly found common ground would prompt him to agree.

"Do we have any other suspects?" asked the vampire. "Because if this turns out to be a normal kidnapping, that Sylvan guy seems a prime candidate if I ever saw one."

I frowned. "I thought you'd want to avoid doing exactly

what that hunter wanted us to. He named names for a reason."

"What else are we supposed to do?" Maurice asked. "I can find the hunter and shake answers out of him if you'd prefer."

"We're here to find a missing kid," Callum said. "Not fight with that Dylan, however tempting it might be."

"Precisely," Tam said. "That's why it's worth talking to witnesses who might have seen Joy before she went missing. The police backed up Dylan's story and said only one person was in the forest at the time of Joy's disappearance. Do any of you have another alternative?"

Unfortunately, I did not. Aside from searching the rest of the forest while Dylan constantly got underfoot, we were out of other options.

"What does Mrs Hutchins think about this newcomer?" asked Callum. "She's the person to ask, isn't she?"

Farley pulled a face. "I don't know about you, but I don't want to freak her out again."

"Mrs Hutchins is worth talking to, certainly," Tam said. "We can go back to her house later, when her husband's home from work, but for now, we'll visit Sylvan. Is everyone all right with that?"

"All right," I said, relenting. "We'll talk to Sylvan, but I wouldn't be surprised if the hunter is there waiting to laugh at us."

"If he is, he'll regret it." Maurice cracked his knuckles. "Where does this guy live?"

"This way." Tam led the way to a cul-de-sac, upon which the forest encroached so thoroughly that it was hard to tell whether the plants sprouting along the street were intentional or nature running amok. No wonder it had been so easy for Joy to walk into the forest the second her parents turned their backs on her.

"Does this guy live *in* the forest?" I ducked under a

branch, not wanting to get clubbed in the face again, as we made our way past the houses and around a huge oak tree that covered the end of the cul-de-sac.

"I guess so." Tam didn't look best pleased at the idea of going into the woods again, but he led us along a dirt track that wove through the trees.

At first, it didn't look like anyone lived out here at all, but then I spied a cottage set apart from the others, nestled between some trees. It scarcely looked big enough for someone to live in; I'd be surprised if it had more than one room inside, and it was made of wood rather than stone like the rest of the houses in the village. A bit of a fire hazard, if you asked me, but then again, so was the whole forest.

"That Sylvan guy better hope nobody lights any matches nearby," Maurice said, evidently having had the same thought. "Is that supposed to be a regular house or a treehouse?"

"Let's see." Tam strode up to the door and knocked firmly on the wooden surface.

The door opened a moment later, revealing a short figure with pointed ears jutting up from his nest of grey hair.

My mouth dropped open. *Oh. He's an elf.* Why hadn't I thought that the reason the house wasn't human sized was because its owner wasn't a human?

Tam paused long enough for me to be sure he'd been surprised, too, but his voice was calm. "Hello. I'm sorry to disturb you."

"This is a surprise." The elf peered up at Tam. "Another one?"

"Another what?" Tam's voice held a sharp edge. "I assume you're Sylvan?"

"That's me." He spied the rest of us and grinned, displaying crooked teeth. "You must be new here too. There are a lot of you, aren't there?"

"Actually, we're visiting," said Tam. "We're here representing the Wardens. I assume you've met the other visitor … Dylan?"

"Yes … a rather unpleasant individual, isn't he? Are you friends?"

"Definitely not," I said firmly. "We're with the Wardens, not the hunters. If you don't mind my asking, how long have you lived here?"

"Oh, about two weeks."

Two weeks. Hmm. I guessed I couldn't fault anyone who might have been suspicious of his arrival, since he seemed to have intentionally picked a house that lay apart from the rest of the village, and he seemed to be the only elf in town too. Glenn hadn't suspected him, though, and we hadn't asked Mr and Mrs Hutchins to share their opinion on him yet.

"Have you met many of the locals?" asked Tam. "Or haven't you had time to introduce yourself?"

"Oh, I expect I've met most of them by now."

Really? Admittedly, the village was small, but he didn't sound entirely sure of himself.

"Including Mr and Mrs Hutchins?" Tam asked carefully. "And their daughter?"

"Ah, yes. Lovely couple… It's a shame their daughter's missing. Have you heard?"

Tension surged in the air, but the elf didn't appear to notice.

"Yes," said Tam. "I heard. I actually wanted to ask you a couple of questions about her—about Joy. If that's okay with you."

"Of course." His vague expression remained intact. "I've already spoken to that Dennis fellow…"

"You mean Dylan?" Tam asked. "Yes, he told us that you were in the forest around the time Joy went missing. Is that true?"

"Well, yes. I'm always in the forest." He laughed to himself, as if enjoying a private joke.

"What's so funny?" Maurice asked from behind me. "A girl went missing in the woods near your house. Think that's a joke, do you?"

"Ah, no, that isn't right," said the elf. "She went missing somewhere over … there."

He pointed in the direction of the Hutchinses' house, which, in fairness, was on the opposite side of the village to his own home.

"We're aware," Tam said. "If you were in the forest at the time, did you see her before she disappeared?"

"I'm afraid I didn't," he said. "The forest is tricky if you aren't prepared, and she certainly wasn't."

"What's that supposed to mean?" Maurice asked. "Did you kidnap her or not?"

"Maurice," Callum hissed.

"Kidnap?" The elf blinked in confusion, apparently oblivious to the warning note in the vampire's voice. "Me? No, no, certainly not."

"Do you know where she is?" Tam pressed. "Is she still in the forest? Her parents are worried for her."

"I'm afraid I have no idea where she is." His brow furrowed. "Her parents are worried? That's concerning."

"They are," I interjected. "That was why they called us to help find her, and it would help if you told us what you knew."

"I thought I did." He retreated back into the hallway. "I wish you the best of luck with your search."

"You weren't any help at all," said Maurice, his voice muffled when Callum put a hand over his mouth.

Without replying, the elf closed the door on us.

"Weird guy," Farley commented. "Do you think he's hiding something?"

"Definitely," said Maurice. "If he isn't hiding that kid inside his fire hazard of a house, I'm a unicorn."

"Nah, we'd have heard if he had a kid tied up in that house," Callum said. "I don't think he's the kidnapper. He's way too out of touch with reality to be scheming to steal children."

"I thought that too," I said. I looked to Tam, but our team leader had gone to examine the forest around the cottage. "Are most elves that eccentric? I thought they usually lived in communities with their own kind."

"That's also true." Callum watched as Tam paced to the left of the cottage and peered into the surrounding trees. "Tam, where are you going?"

"Did you see someone in the woods?" He didn't respond, making the skin on the back of my neck prickle. "Tam?"

"No." He swivelled back to us, his shoulders tense. "All of you—wait for me in the village. I'll follow you in a minute."

My heart skipped a beat. "Why?"

"Are you sure?" Callum asked. "We can help you. I thought we were going to search the woods."

"There's nothing else to do in the village," Farley put in. "Unless you want us to talk to the police again."

"Yes … perhaps you should."

"Tam, what's going on?" I tried to catch his eye, but his attention remained on the trees. I followed his gaze in an attempt to see what had got him so rattled, and my gaze snagged on the path behind us. "Erm … wasn't there an oak tree there?"

"Yeah…" Callum strode across the clearing to the path through which we'd entered. "There was. Where'd it go?"

"I think you mean, where'd *we* go?" Farley said quietly. "I don't see the village. Do you?"

I peered through the trees. She was right. The houses

were nowhere to be seen—and when I whipped back around to Tam, the elf's house had disappeared as well.

"What the hell is going on?" I backed up a few steps, certain the house should be right there. I'd only looked away for a few seconds, but the elf's home might as well have never existed at all.

"What's this?" Callum stared around, wide eyed. "Where are we?"

"We're still in the forest, right?" Farley edged closer to him. "Is this a … a spell?"

After a long pause, Tam said, "It must be. I'm sorry. I should have spotted it sooner."

"None of us saw anything either." What kind of spell could cause us to end up in another part of the forest altogether, much less make the elf's house disappear? I spied a path branching off and started walking that way, but Tam caught my arm.

"Watch out." He released me before it had quite registered that he'd grabbed me. "We shouldn't split up. If the forest's playing tricks on us, we need to stick together."

My skin tingled on the spot where he'd touched me, but urgency overwhelmed any other instinct. "All right."

"What's that mean?" His expression darkening, Maurice swivelled to our team leader. "We're trapped?"

"There'll be a way out," Tam said. "But I don't know where it is."

Unease skittered down my spine. I'd never heard him admit to not knowing something before. What was this spell, to have escaped our team leader's attention until it was too late?

"We're trapped in the forest," said Maurice. "Bloody great."

"We aren't trapped." Callum confidently strode down the path that should have led to the village. "We're bound to find the way out eventually if we keep walking, right? The forest doesn't go on forever."

I didn't share his optimism, but Tam's comment about staying together came to mind. "Tam, should we head that way? We need to start somewhere."

"Yes … you're right." He overtook Callum and led the way out of the clearing.

We followed the path for several minutes in a tense silence, and then I came to a sudden stop. "Wait. Joy isn't still lost in here, is she? Was this where she went?"

"It wouldn't surprise me," Tam said in a low voice. "Everyone, keep an eye out for her while we're walking."

"Of course," Callum said. "I should have thought of that too."

"I already did," Maurice said, though his tone held none of its usual cockiness, and I didn't have the inclination to call him out on a lie when we had other priorities.

Another period of quietness passed.

Later, Farley asked, "How'd someone put a spell on the whole forest? More to the point, why?"

"A prank?" I suggested. "The spell can't cover the whole forest, surely."

"It doesn't have to." Maurice irritably gestured to the trees ahead of us. "What if we're stuck in a loop and are going in circles?"

"We aren't going in circles." Tam kept walking, but if the path did loop, I couldn't tell where it ended or began. We might as well have been in the wilderness, away from civilisation altogether.

"Screw this." Maurice took an abrupt turn off the path and climbed the leaf-strewn slope on our left. "Maybe the point is to keep us stuck on the path when the way out is through the trees instead."

"That's possible." Tam halted, his gaze flickering to the left and right. "This way looks the most promising."

He turned right and descended a slope that led downhill between the trees, while the rest of us tried not to slip in the mud coating the leaves at our feet. When we reached the foot of the slope, Farley slid into a bramble bush, and it was Callum's turn to hit his head on a branch when he came to her rescue.

"Ow." He helped Farley disentangle herself from the mess of brambles, under which lay a mass of vibrant-looking wild toadstools. "Hey, at least we have something to eat if we get stuck here for too long."

"Those are poisonous, I'm betting," said Farley. "Hey—what is it, Tam?"

Tam had gone still a short distance away, his gaze fixed at a point among the trees—then his ears pricked. "I hear someone."

"You do?" I didn't hear anything, but I doubted Tam would have reacted to nothing at all. "Is it Joy?"

"I don't think so." Tam waited for us to catch up before leading us onward through the maze of trees. Within a minute, I heard the distinct murmur of human chatter.

"Civilisation!" Callum bounded ahead, and the rest of us picked up speed when we saw the stone houses amid the trees.

Finally, we stepped out of the woods and into a street that seemed considerably emptier than it had been earlier. Nobody appeared to be outside, while darkness swathed the streets between streetlamps that hadn't been lit the last time I'd seen them. Weird. Hadn't it been morning when we'd set out? The sun wasn't supposed to set until eight or nine o'clock at night at this time of year.

"What's going on?" Farley's gaze went up to the sky. "It can't be evening already."

"Did we travel through time?" Callum stepped around a streetlamp. "Or is it a side effect of that weird spell?"

"What kind of spell can make us experience time on fast-forward?" I looked to Tam, who looked grim again. "We definitely weren't in there for more than half an hour or so."

"Excuse me—what time is it?" Callum flagged down a lone elderly man walking outside, who eyed him with suspicion.

"Ten o'clock at night," the old man answered promptly. "You should go home. It's not wise to be out after dark in times like these."

Chills raced down my back as I watched him depart. How could it be ten at night? Magic couldn't mess with the passage of time. I thought that was a fundamental rule, though I'd freely admit I wasn't an expert.

"What are we supposed to do now?" Maurice scowled. "If he's telling the truth, we've wasted the whole day and have nothing to show for it."

"Not necessarily," said Tam. "We can still talk to the police again … and Mrs Hutchins too. I think it's worth asking her if she's met Sylvan."

"And if she knows the forest is under a spell," I added.

Of course, by now, her husband would have been at home for ages. They also might not be thrilled at us disturbing them at night, but it couldn't be helped. We didn't know what else had happened in the interim since we'd been in the forest, and besides, Mrs Hutchins deserved to know about the spell … especially if her daughter might have fallen into the same trap.

Tam walked the short distance to the Hutchinses' house first and knocked on the door. The curtains were drawn across the living room windows, which at least meant I couldn't see the crystal ball, but the light of a lamp showed that someone was still awake.

The door swung inward, and a balding man surveyed our group with suspicion. "Who are you?"

Farley took a step back from the hostility radiating from the man's voice, but the rest of us held our ground.

"We're here to help find Joy," said Tam. "Your wife called us."

"You're lying," he said. "My wife certainly didn't call you."

"Didn't she tell you we visited earlier?" Tam asked. "We went to look around the forest."

"Wade?" I heard Mrs Hutchins's voice from behind her husband. "What is it?"

"These ruffians claim you called them to town."

"Oh!" She peered over her husband's shoulder. "Yes—don't worry, Wade. They're the Wardens I called."

"Wardens?" he echoed in sceptical tones. "How is that different to the other one?"

The other one... "Did you meet Dylan, by any chance? The paranormal hunter? Because we're not with him."

Some of the hostility faded from his expression. "You aren't?"

"Definitely not," I asserted. "The police called him, but your wife was the one who contacted us to help find your daughter. We wanted to give her an update on our search."

"Yes … you went out this morning," she said.

Mr. Hutchins surveyed our group. "Did you find anything?"

"No," said Tam, "but we did encounter something unusual in the forest. We went to visit Sylvan—a local who moved to town recently. Have you met him?"

"Oh, the old man?" said Mr Hutchins. "He seems nice, though a little absentminded."

He doesn't suspect him, then?

"When we left his house, we walked into a spell." I got to the point. "The village disappeared, and we couldn't find our way back. When we finally got out, it was night. We lost a whole day in there."

"You did?" Mr Hutchins's brow furrowed. "The forest can be confusing to navigate, certainly, especially in the darkness."

"It wasn't night when we left," Tam said. "I believe we walked into a spell, like Perry said. Have you or anyone else experienced anything of the sort recently?"

"I don't know of such a thing," said Mr Hutchins. "A spell, on our forest? Seems unlikely. Someone would have noticed."

That was true enough, but how could people who *lived* here be completely unaware of the spell's existence?

"We think it might be connected to Joy's disappearance," Tam said. "If she walked into a similar trap, it would explain why nobody has been able to find her. We were lucky to get out."

"It's news to me," said Mr Hutchins. I tried to see his wife's expression, but she'd retreated into the living room without expressing her own thoughts on the matter. "You didn't find any signs of Joy in there?"

"Unfortunately not," said Tam. "I hope we can bring you answers soon."

"So do I," he said. "Will you be staying in the village tonight?"

"No, but we'll be back as soon as it's light." Tam stepped back from the door. "We'll see you soon."

As Mr Hutchins closed the door, I turned to my teammates. "Does it strike any of you as odd that he didn't notice a spell right next to the village?"

"Not if he doesn't go into the woods much," Callum said.

"His daughter did vanish in there," said Farley. "And he seemed on edge when he first saw us. I think he and Dylan had an argument."

"I figured that too." I swivelled towards Tam, who focused

on the trees shadowing the houses from behind. "Do you reckon he's still around? Dylan?"

"He's probably gone home by now," said Callum. "He wouldn't have wanted to stay overnight."

"Don't hunters normally camp on missions?" Maurice said. "I'll have a look on the way back."

"Can you imagine camping in that forest?" I turned my back on the Hutchinses' house with a shiver. "On that note—did *he* know about the spell? Was that why he sent us to talk to Sylvan?"

"Good question." Tam's attention sharpened. "Either way, we'll definitely have to talk to Dylan again."

Yeah. If the hunter knew that the forest contained a spell designed to trap anyone who walked in, did he know the source? Had he simply been trying to get rid of us—or had he been trying to do worse?

6

"We're not going back to the tower already, are we?" Callum asked Tam as he began to walk away from the Hutchinses' house. "What if another kid gets taken overnight?"

"Taken by whom?" Maurice said. "It sounds like Joy walked into the forest by herself. We haven't seen any signs that anyone or anything captured her."

That was true. While leaving the village made guilt twinge inside my chest, I also wasn't very keen on the idea of doing any more sleuthing by night. We'd been lucky enough to escape the forest's trap once already, and it'd be even harder to navigate without any light.

"I don't like the idea of her being out there on her own." Farley echoed my thoughts. "I wish we could do something."

"It's not ideal," Tam said, "but there's nothing we can do until we can discern the nature of that spell. I think it's better for us to go back to the tower and have a look at our notes. Maybe contact the office and see if they've recorded anything similar in past missions."

"Sounds like a plan." We might have failed to find Joy, but

we wouldn't do any good by getting ourselves lost again either. Even from here under the soft light of the streetlamps, the trees shrouding the village had taken on a decidedly sinister air. I didn't envy Maurice for having to walk back through the trees, but a vampire at least had the ability to make his journey a short one.

"Maurice." Tam faced the vampire. "Don't take this the wrong way, but I don't think it's a good idea for you to walk back alone."

"I'm not scared of the dark," he growled. "As if any self-respecting vampire would let a forest scare them off."

"You don't want to get lost again, do you?" Callum asked him. "Wouldn't you rather use a transportation spell and get it over with?"

"Even falling in a puddle is better than getting lost in there for days," I put in. "Not that I was planning to land in one. As I told you, I did that by accident—"

Maurice vanished in a blur of speed. Tam sighed. "I thought he'd do that."

"Typical." I shook my head. "He'd better hope he doesn't take any wrong turns."

"He should be fine as long as he avoids Sylvan's house," said Callum. "Ah—does *he* know about the spell? You'd think he would, since it's on his doorstep."

"He wasn't all there, though," Farley put in.

Tam's gaze darkened. "I hope Maurice knows what he's doing. Perry, are you ready?"

"Ready." My heart skipped a little, though I knew he was just asking me to get out my wand. "Ah, is everyone else ready to leave?"

"Definitely," said Callum, and the others murmured agreement.

Wand in hand, I cast a transportation spell on our group. In moments, gravel replaced the dirt path underneath our feet, and the dark windows of houses were replaced with the equally dark tower windows. I shivered, my gaze drawn unwillingly to the mass of trees next to the castle.

"Maurice didn't beat us back this time," Callum observed, while Tam unlocked the front door. "Is he okay?"

"He will be," Tam said over his shoulder as he beckoned us inside.

We entered the tower, happy to retreat into the living room with its warm fireplace and comfy chairs. Yet it was hard to ignore the guilt that Joy would be unable to experience the same, and our sojourn in the forest had left me decidedly ill at ease.

After we'd all settled into armchairs in the living room, I asked, "Where's Maurice? He didn't get lost in the forest again, did he?"

"I hope not." Tam, who hadn't sat down, paced around the backs of the chairs. "I'll keep an eye out for him."

"Do our files say anything about creepy spells that cause people to lose track of time?" Farley lifted her phone. "Dammit—no signal again. Or any internet connection."

"Seriously?" Without a phone signal or internet, we couldn't reach Maurice if he was lost somewhere out of reach. I also couldn't call Kellen, who was my go-to whenever I had a question that might require him to poke into the Wardens' records. "It's not even raining."

"The signal's temperamental out here. You know that." Tam's pacing did not help my nerves, and Farley had hunched up into a ball in the chair next to mine.

"Maurice is fine," said Callum, his voice confident. "If anything, we should be worried that he ran into that hunter again on the way back. Worried for the hunter, that is."

"He might have," I acknowledged. "I can't imagine anyone wanting to camp in the woods, but hunters are weird."

"Dylan must know about that spell," said Farley. "There's no way he can't have seen it, if he's been there for days."

"I can't imagine that guy admitting to getting lost in the woods," said Callum. "I wouldn't have known we'd walked into a trap if you hadn't pointed it out, Tam."

My gaze swung to the team leader, who'd halted next to the darkened window, presumably to keep an eye out for Maurice. I might have joined him, if not for the spiderwebs covering the glass and the threat of one of their occupants landing on my head, which had occurred the last time I'd tried to peer out of that window.

"The spell couldn't have been there very long, or else more villagers would have noticed," I commented. "Though it's safe to say that poor kid's disappearance is probably connected."

We hadn't heard or seen any signs of her while we were lost in the forest ourselves, but we had no idea how far the spell stretched, and we might have been stuck in there all night if we'd continued looking. Or longer. I'd never heard of a spell with that effect, and although I hadn't exactly studied the subject in depth, it wasn't supposed to be possible to use magic to affect the passage of time. Unless the Wardens had a secret time-travel division that I was unaware of, but I had my doubts.

No, the spell must have another explanation—but killing a monster was child's play compared to dealing with a spell that none of us could see or control.

Nobody spoke for a while, until the sound of a door opening downstairs made everyone startle—except for Tam. "It's Maurice."

"How do you know?"

The door to the living room opened an instant later, and the vampire entered. *Right. He's the fastest person in the castle.*

"Did you get lost on the way back?" I asked him.

Maurice glided to an unoccupied chair. "No."

"Did you stop to look around?"

The vampire lounged in the chair and propped his legs on a footstool. "You're nosy, aren't you? Or were you worried about me?"

Annoyance replaced any hints of relief that might have arisen upon his return. "I'm worried about the missing kid being stuck in that creepy forest. That was what was on my mind. Not whatever you were doing in the woods that was more important than searching for her."

He lifted his head. "Not that it's any of your business, but I went to check up on our hunter friend. He's camping out there in the woods. Has a tent and everything."

"Wait, seriously?" Callum raised a brow. "Isn't he worried he'll get lost? Or walk into the spell?"

"I bet he already knows how to avoid it." The hunter likely hadn't cast the spell, but I had a hard time believing he was unaware of its existence. "And he's too much of a fool to be afraid of monsters."

"He knew?" Farley queried. "You don't think he cast the spell himself, do you?"

"I doubt he has a magical bone in his body," said Maurice scathingly. "He just wanted us off his hands."

"Is he even trying to find the missing kid, though?" asked Farley. "I couldn't get a handle on his feelings, but he didn't seem worried on Joy's behalf. Not in the slightest."

"Not as worried as he was about getting rid of us." I glanced at Tam, who'd remained near the window despite the vampire's return. "I wonder if it's worth calling his bosses and letting them know one of their people is causing trouble?"

Tam shook his head. "I don't know which branch of the hunters he's from, but they don't tend to check up on their people. They're not as into paperwork as the Wardens are."

"Figures." The hunters were more interested in how many paranormal criminals they could take down than anything else, and they didn't care if their targets were necessarily guilty either. Yet another reason we'd clashed in the past … but why would they have sent someone to find a missing kid if he had no intention of doing his job? "Does he have nothing better to do with his time than go on a camping trip?"

"Apparently not," said Callum. "We can't call his bosses while we have no signal, anyway."

"True, but I don't trust him." We all agreed on that, even Maurice, but figuring out how far the hunter's knowledge stretched would have to wait until tomorrow. "You didn't do anything to him, did you, Maurice?"

"Tempting, but no," he said. "He was armed. I didn't want a stake in the back."

"Wise idea," said Callum. "He seemed the jumpy sort."

"I hoped we might be able to reach an agreement with him," Tam said. "Finding Joy is the priority. That's what we have to focus on tomorrow."

"Of course," I said. "If Dylan is actively working against us, though, it's a problem."

"Yeah." Farley turned to address Tam. "I don't want to fight with him, either, but he might have been trying to get us lost in the forest so he'd get the credit for finding the missing kid."

"That's possible," Tam agreed. "I'd like to avoid provoking him, though, at least until we can find out the extent of his own knowledge. He's camping in the forest, which suggests he doesn't feel threatened by whatever might be in there."

"That or he's missing a few brain cells," said Callum. "I don't trust him, either, but I can't imagine a hunter casting a spell that complex even if he had the talent. I'll say he probably knows it's there, but I don't know if he's already walked into it himself."

"If he had, did he tell the police?" I thought back to Glenn's general unhelpfulness. "You'd think Glenn would have noticed people kept getting lost in the woods, though he's almost as dopey as that elf."

"Oh, Glenn doesn't know anything," Maurice said. "The girl's parents, though? *They* might."

"You think they do?" Mr Hutchins hadn't seemed to have a clue what we were talking about, but his wife was a Seer. If she knew about the spell, I couldn't think why she wouldn't have warned us. Didn't she want us to find her child?

Tam left the window and crossed the room without acknowledging my question. I shifted in my seat, watching as he pushed the door closed behind him. The soft sound of footsteps on the stairs followed.

"Is it just me, or is he being more evasive than usual?" I whispered to the others.

"Not just you." Farley watched the doorway. "He seems … preoccupied."

"Can you blame him?" Callum indicated Maurice. "He was worried because one of our team decided to ignore his instructions and walk straight through the cursed forest without any cares."

"I told him I'd be fine," the vampire shot back. "I'm not the one who's bothering him."

"Then what?" I asked, not expecting an answer.

"It's not like I can get into his head, is it?" Maurice scowled. "I've no more clue what he's thinking than the rest of you. Stop badgering me."

That was true, since Tam had supposedly trained himself to keep his mind from being read by vampires. I was more inclined to think that Maurice avoided peering into his thoughts out of politeness—or at least respect for his team leader, a courtesy he extended to nobody else—but at his words, curiosity rose inside me like a tidal wave. Did Tam know something that he wasn't telling the rest of us? He was the team leader, the decision maker, and usually the person we trusted to keep everything together. His current unease made *me* uneasy, which did not bode well for our mission— or our ability to find the missing child.

I rose to my feet, but as I made for the door, Maurice appeared in front of me in a blur. I had to grab the back of a chair to avoid walking straight into him. "What are you doing?"

"Stopping you from making a fool of yourself."

Heat rushed to my face. "What's that supposed to mean?"

"What I said," he said. "If Tam wants us to know anything, he'll tell us directly. You're wasting your time otherwise."

"Who are you to speak for him?" An irrational anger rose within me. "As you just pointed out yourself, you can't read his mind any more than the rest of us can."

I hadn't been intending that as a slight—not entirely—but the vampire sidestepped me with a shrug. "Fine, follow him if you like. Just remember who the team leader is."

"I'm perfectly aware of that." I returned to my seat, grudgingly. "You're the one who seems to have trouble remembering."

Callum and Farley frowned at the vampire, but they didn't contradict him either. Who knew, maybe Tam had a theory he wanted to check against his notes before he shared it with us, and if even the vampire couldn't penetrate his thoughts, why would I assume I'd be the one he'd confide in? I was the newbie, and Tam had known the others far longer than he'd known me.

Besides, I had little doubt that he'd have a plan. He always did.

———

The following day, I woke at dawn and went for my usual morning run to clear my head. I intentionally stuck to paths that didn't go near the woods, not keen on the idea of entering another forest after yesterday's misadventures. I hadn't slept particularly well, but that was to be expected after we'd skipped forward in time a day. No doubt I was experiencing something akin to magical jet lag. If that existed.

When I jogged back to the tower, I spied Tam waiting outside, and my heart did a treacherous skip inside my chest. *None of that, Perry.* I hadn't seen him much since our return to the tower yesterday; he'd been in the downstairs office most of the night, and I wasn't sure he'd even slept.

"Hey." I halted at the doors, wishing I'd had time to clean myself up so he didn't have to see me breathless and drenched in sweat from my run. "Something up?"

"You didn't go into the woods, did you?"

"Wasn't keen on the idea after yesterday." Had he thought I would? The thought that he might have been worried about me warmed me despite the circumstances. "Ah—do we have a phone signal today?"

"Not yet." He withdrew into the tower, while I surreptitiously fixed my hair and checked my reflection in Maurice's car's wing mirror before following Tam inside.

The door at the foot of the stairs lay slightly open, revealing the room the team used as a cross between an office and gymnasium. Inside, Tam picked up one of the sharpened sticks he usually carried and began performing exercises with speed and finesse that drew my attention despite my best efforts, my gaze captured by the play of muscles under his thin shirt.

Tam caught me looking and tilted his head. "Perry? Did

you want to come in?"

"Yeah…" I sidled into the room, not smooth at all, but I'd completely forgotten what I'd intended to ask him. Squashing down a sudden rush of self-consciousness, I reached the nearest punching bag and gave it a couple of half hearted punches. "I don't know that I'll need to use weapons this time around. How do you fight a monster you can't see?"

"How indeed," he murmured, continuing to twirl the stick while I did my level best not to stare at him. Honestly, what was the matter with me? I'd wanted to talk to him alone since yesterday, and ordinarily, I wouldn't have an issue voicing what was on my mind, but the case had left me with such a tangle of questions that it was hard to pry a thread loose and focus on it. My suspicion that he'd blamed himself as team leader for getting us all lost in the forest might be easier to put into words, but what could I even add? That I understood? I didn't, not really. I'd never headed a team, and I'd only ever been responsible for myself.

Maybe that's my problem. "Where'd you learn to fight?"

"Huh?" He executed a complicated manoeuvre that should by rights have caused him to drop the stick, but he caught it between his fingertips with apparent ease. "I grew up learning martial arts so I could learn to defend myself."

Why would you need to? The question lodged in my throat, unable to escape. I didn't know much about his history at all, except that he'd been in the Wardens since he was a teenager. Like me. He hadn't pushed me to share my own past, so I didn't want to blurt out my other thought, which was that he didn't tick the boxes of any other paranormal I could think of. 'What are you?' wasn't a polite question to ask at the best of times, and while I'd normally default to wizard or shifter, neither fit him. His speed and dexterity put me in mind of a vampire, but that wasn't right either.

Conscious that he was waiting for a reply, I said, "I never

thought a stick could be that lethal."

"I thought you said anything could be a weapon if you had the imagination."

A smile came to my lips. "I did say that, yes."

When he smiled back, I swore the blood in my veins started fizzing like an overflowing can of cola. Flustered, I turned away and hit the punching bag a few times, pretending to be oblivious to his presence behind me and wishing the downstairs room had a window I could open. It was entirely too hot in here.

After a painfully long moment, the rustle of paper across the room drew my attention. I swivelled on my heel and then stumbled when the bag hit me in the side. *Again—smooth, Perry.* Tam, who leaned against the desk with his head buried in a folder, didn't notice my misstep, for a mercy.

"What's that?" I asked. "The case folder?"

He lifted his head. "Yes ... I wish they'd given us more information."

"Me too." I steadied the punching bag with my hand. "They didn't mention the spell on the forest ... or that someone called the hunters before they called us."

"The Wardens don't normally mention if other people are investigating unless they belong to the Wardens themselves." He put down the folder. "Dylan isn't the one who concerns me ... Clementine is."

"Who?"

"Mrs Hutchins."

My thoughts went back to our second visit to the Hutchinses' house the previous evening. "You think she knew about the spell?"

"I think it's unlikely that a Seer would be unaware of strange magical interference," he replied. "And I'm not sure her husband was honest about his own lack of knowledge either."

"Aren't you?" I considered this. "Seers sometimes do things based on a vague vision of the future that they can't necessarily put into words, but I don't know that a spell like that would have been easy to spot in a vision either. The forest looked normal."

Except that we hadn't been able to get out—until Tam had somehow picked up on our proximity to the village. I still didn't know how he'd done that, though his instincts were sharper than almost anyone's I'd known.

"Have you met many?"

"What?" My mind blanked when he looked directly at me. "Oh. You mean Seers? A few, but they don't tend to stay in the same room as me for long."

When his attention remained steady, I felt myself flush. It'd briefly slipped my memory that Tam had also witnessed Mrs Hutchins's terrified reaction upon seeing me, and as he began to reply, I blurted, "I don't mind. I mean, I do, but her kid disappeared. That's the important thing here. Not my curse."

I didn't need him to express pity and was relieved when he simply nodded. "Her ability as a Seer might have given her more insight that can point at the cause of the spell on the forest," he said. "It's certainly worth asking more questions later."

"Yeah…" I trailed off, thinking of the crystal ball. "Have *you* met any Seers before?"

"No more than the average person," he said. "It's a rare gift, and I wonder if it wasn't coincidental that it was her child that was taken and not someone else's."

"Taken?" I didn't know why, but hearing him say 'taken' and not 'disappeared' made unease stir inside me. Perhaps because Mr Hutchins had used the same word himself. "By whom, though?"

He shook his head. "It's all speculation, like I said."

Is it? I squashed down my disquiet, recalling another question that had come to mind during my night of insomnia. "Have you ever met an elf before?"

"Once or twice, yes."

"Are they normally as clueless as Sylvan is?"

"Sometimes," he said, his gaze on the desk instead of on me. "They vary as much as humans do."

"Of course." I tried to catch his eye but failed. "I just meant—did you think Sylvan was acting suspiciously enough to have taken the kid?"

"I wouldn't take anything a paranormal hunter said seriously."

I might have said the same, but something was undeniably weird about the spell's proximity to Sylvan's house and the timing of his arrival in town. "I guess. He's the only newcomer in town and a possible witness—not to mention the spell was right next to his part of the forest—so I've wondered if he might know something else."

"He might." He moved towards the door. "But it's not worth the risk of getting caught in the spell again. I think we should avoid that part of the forest."

What? "Until we've figured out how far it stretches? What if Joy is in there somewhere?"

"She might be," he acknowledged, "but until we know for sure, we're better off keeping our distance."

"If you're sure." I forced out one of the questions cluttering my thoughts. "Tam—do you have a theory about who took her? Joy, I mean?"

"No." He didn't look at me. "Not yet."

He's lying. But he'd already left the room, leaving me staring at the back of the door as it swung closed behind him. *But why, exactly?*

7

Tam's odd behaviour weighed on my mind as I went upstairs to shower and waited for the others to wake up. They typically rose much later than I did —especially Maurice—so I ended up going back downstairs to the office for the lack of anything else to do. In theory, the downstairs room was supposed to have better internet connection than the rest of the tower, but my attempts to get onto the Wizarding Web were met with a resounding failure.

Tam must have gone outside or up to his own room, because he wasn't in the office. He'd left the folder on the desk, though, and I had a brief flick through it before my gaze caught on the noticeboard above. Unusually, it was empty, containing no maps or anything pertaining to the current case. While we didn't really *have* anything to pin there—though a map of the forest would have come in handy, now that I thought about it—it was a reminder of the ways this case departed from our usual routine.

Admittedly, we hadn't done enough missions as a group to have an established 'usual routine,' and every case was unique, but the lack of any visible progress bugged me almost as much as Tam's secrecy did. We might be certain that Joy was lost in the forest, but we didn't know the first thing about the spell, nor whether it was the sort of task that required the Wardens' expertise at all. Of course, it would help if we could get a bloody signal so I could call Kellen and ask for his guidance.

Hearing footsteps above, I left the room and climbed the stairs back to the main floor. There, I found a bleary-eyed Callum shambling around the kitchen, dressed in a pair of battered stripy pyjamas that had been repaired enough times that I assumed he'd shifted into a wolf while wearing them at least once. Possibly while sleeping.

"I'll make coffee," I offered. "I didn't realise anyone else was up. Except Tam, that is."

"Is he downstairs?" He stepped aside to let me reach the kettle, his eyes half-closed, and bumped into the work surface. Glad I hadn't let him try to make the coffee on his own, I filled the kettle with water.

"No… I guess he's out." I set the kettle back into place and flicked the switch. "He's acting even weirder than yesterday, if that's possible."

"Weird how?" He yawned, reaching into the cupboard and pulling out a loaf of bread. "Did the phone signal come back?"

"No." I watched the water in the kettle boil, unable to put my unease into words. "He's just being … evasive. I'm sure he has theories about who took Joy, but he wouldn't tell me."

"He might not know. I sure don't." He yawned again as he stuck a couple of slices of bread into the toaster. "I also slept like crap. Kept dreaming about that creepy forest."

"I guess that's got all of us on edge," I acknowledged as the kettle's whistling reached a higher pitch. "But … he's not acting like himself. I know we haven't done that many missions as a team, but he's usually more on top of things than this. He hasn't even updated the noticeboard down-stairs, or got out any past records, or…"

"We've only been on the case for a day," he reminded me. "We've had no internet access either. It's not like we've found any clues that we can look up, like monster footprints we can compare to past missions."

"Never thought I'd be weirded out by the lack of monster footprints." I grabbed a few mugs and set about making coffee for everyone except Farley, who preferred tea. And Maurice, whose bags of blood in the fridge greeted me when I went to get the milk.

"It's possible that the girl was taken by a human, not a monster." Callum accepted a mug of coffee from me with a grateful nod. "Such as whoever cast that spell. That was no monster."

"Yeah." When the toast popped up, I passed each slice to Callum and stuck two more slices in the toaster. "Is there anything in the records about time-warping spells, do you think?"

"I doubt it." The answer came from Farley, who'd entered the kitchen dressed in rabbit-patterned pyjamas and a pair of fluffy slippers. "If it's possible at all, it's the sort of informa-tion the Wardens would keep under lock and key at their offices."

"And we have no way to reach them." Callum helped me carry the other coffee mugs to the table and gave the sole cup of tea to Farley. "Not that that's anything new."

"It's a bloody pain." I returned to the kitchen and loaded the toaster again. "Farley, do *you* think Tam's acting weirdly?"

"In what way?"

"She was worried that Tam hadn't updated the notice-board," Callum told her. "He doesn't always, does he? During our last case, we weren't staying at the castle, so he didn't need to."

"That's true." Farley picked an apple from the fruit bowl on the table and took a bite. "We also don't have a map this time. Pity, because it would help with navigating the forest."

"I thought the same, but I doubt that spell will show up on a map." I fished a box of cereal out of the cupboard and carried that to the table too. "Tam said we should avoid going near it. He was pretty insistent, in fact."

"When was this?" asked Callum curiously.

"We had a brief chat earlier while we were in the weapons room." Heat rose to my cheeks at the memory, and I concentrated on getting plates and bowls out of the cupboard to hide my face from the others. "I was lamenting not being able to just stab whatever took Joy captive and be done with it."

"You don't think it's a monster?" Farley bounded up and helped me carry a stack of plates. "An invisible one that doesn't leave prints?"

"It's not impossible, is it?" I put down the plates, mildly frustrated that I hadn't convinced either of them that Tam's behaviour was anything out of the ordinary. "Especially if it's hiding in the spelled part of the forest and Joy walked in there of her own accord without being taken captive at all."

"Who created it, though?" Farley grabbed a bowl and poured out cereal for herself. "Someone must have cast the spell, and I thought it was impossible to use magic to mess with the passage of time. Granted, I dropped out of magical education before I was sixteen."

"Same here." Not that I'd been the best student anyway. "Whatever kind of spell it is, I can't think why someone from the village would have bewitched their own forest. Who else did it, though?"

"Wait." Callum's eyes widened. She was suddenly awake. "Do elves have magic?"

"They might." Farley stared at him from across the table. "Of course."

"Are *they* in our records?" I grabbed my phone and opened the basic file of information I'd received from the Wardens. It might not contain much more than the fundamentals on the most common magical monsters, but elves were common enough, right? More so than demons, certainly.

"I have no idea." Callum munched toast, looking preoccupied. "They aren't monsters…"

"No." They weren't monsters, not the sort we usually hunted. Like goblins and ogres, elves didn't *look* human and consequently tended to live apart from other paranormals, but that didn't make them villains by default. I of all people knew better than to judge anyone based on their appearance or anything else they couldn't control.

Yet that spell on the forest … where else might it have come from?

I skimmed through the contents page and snagged on the letter *E*. "Yeah … elves are in here."

"What's it say?" Farley leaned forward. "They're not classed as monsters, surely."

"No…" I skimmed the text, and my heart sank. "No, but it just says they're around four feet tall and have pointed ears. And that they tend to prefer to live in colonies in forests, away from humans."

"Does it mention their magic?" asked Callum.

"No." Disgruntled, I skipped to the end. "I might as well have checked Witchipedia for all the good that did."

"Nothing at all?" Farley slumped in her seat. "There's got to be more information downstairs, surely."

I picked up my coffee mug. "They keep to themselves, I guess. I can ask Kellen if the office has more information when we finally get a signal. Maybe we can stop somewhere on the way to the village and try again."

"Good call," said Callum.

I skimmed back through the file with one hand as I drank my coffee, pausing to reread a sentence or two.

"The legends mention elves in connection with capturing human children," I read. "Granted, that's folklore passed around by normals, which usually isn't accurate."

"Not that unusual." Callum chewed more toast. "The file on 'vampires' is pretty sparse too."

"Damn right." Maurice rested his elbow on the door-frame, a faint breeze stirring up at his arrival. "Are you causing trouble again?"

"Trouble?" I put down my mug and reached for a slice of toast. "No, I'm just checking the basic files. We were talking about whether elves had magic."

He snorted. "Of course they have magic."

"The details aren't in our records." I placed my phone on the table, needing both hands to slather margarine and jam onto my toast. "Which is understandable, given how secretive they seem to be ... but if it's possible for them to put a spell on the forest to get people lost, it seems pertinent."

"Yeah ... it does." Farley glanced towards Maurice. "Could you read his mind? Sylvan's, I mean?"

He shot her a sarcastic glance. "I don't read minds without permission, remember?"

"I thought you made exceptions in special circumstances." I took a bite of margarine- and jam-covered toast. "What about Dylan? The hunter? Did you read his thoughts when you saw him setting up camp in the forest?"

"No, but I didn't need to." The vampire eyed the table. "I notice you brought Tam coffee and not me."

"I'm not touching your bottles of rat blood," I informed him. "I don't want to catch a disease. Also, I thought Tam told you that you were free to dive into the hunter's thoughts if necessary."

"It's not rat blood. I get that from the source."

"I didn't need to know that." Farley dropped her cereal spoon back into the bowl. "She's right, you know. You could peer into Dylan's thoughts and confirm if he knew about the spell."

"You think he did?" Callum asked.

"Obviously," Maurice said, his tone dripping with derision. "He wants to find the girl himself and take all the credit. If he gets to take down a team of misfits in the process, all the better."

Unfortunately, Maurice was probably right on that one. Whether the hunter knew about the spell or not didn't necessarily matter, but if he had any idea how to get rid of it…

"We can check with Tam and confirm you have permission to read Dylan's thoughts," I said. "That'll probably be quicker than trying to get the hunter to tell us anything directly."

"Why are you so fixated on me reading minds?" Maurice glowered at me as he walked to the fridge. "I'm not an attack dog you can unleash on anyone who annoys you."

"You know perfectly well that wasn't what I meant." I sipped my coffee, wishing he wouldn't go out of his way to be difficult. Considering how willing he'd been to jump into *my* thoughts when I'd moved into the tower, you'd think he'd have delved straight into the hunter's mind the instant he set eyes on him.

Maurice called me a rude name. *Vampires. Honestly.*

I changed the subject before he got any more wound up. "Do you think there's a way to get to Sylvan's house and question him again without walking straight into that spell?"

"There must be, if other people in the village have met him," said Callum. "He has to leave his house sometimes."

"You'd think," Farley said. "I can't imagine the locals are friendly with him, given their reaction to us showing up. Small communities like that aren't usually welcoming of outsiders."

"Bit of a generalisation," Callum commented. "Technically, he's not an outsider. He lives there, and we don't."

"He's lived there for two weeks," I said. The question was, when exactly had the spell been cast on the forest? I didn't want to jump to the conclusion that the elf had been responsible, but our lack of knowledge about his magical abilities didn't make him look any less suspicious. "Tam thinks he's innocent, but I don't know how we're supposed to ask him any more questions without getting ourselves stuck in the forest for hours again."

"Count me out," said Maurice, departing the kitchen with a flask of dark-red liquid in hand.

What we really needed was our team leader's input, but I could only assume Tam had gone out to the local village, because he hadn't come in to talk to us yet. "I hope he has a plan."

"Who, Tam?" Callum asked. "Of course he'll have a plan."

"He didn't mention one earlier." I picked up my phone and began skimming through the files again. "I'll have to tell him about the elf's magic when he gets back from … from wherever he is."

"He's probably running errands." Callum yawned. "I'm getting more coffee. Want some?"

"Please." My phone pinged, and I dropped it onto my plate. "Yes! I have a signal."

"Assuming you didn't get crumbs inside it," Farley said wryly as I retrieved my phone and wiped sticky crumbs off the screen with a paper towel. "What're you doing? Messaging Kellen?"

"You bet." Not wanting to risk the signal disappearing again, I fired off a quick message to Kellen asking if the Wardens' offices had any more information on elves. Whether he'd have time to reply before we left for the mission or even before the signal disappeared again was debatable, but it was nice to have a bit of luck. "It's worth seeing if the office has anything in their files. I wonder if Tam knows?"

"Do I know what?"

I jumped; Tam himself had entered the kitchen almost as stealthily as a vampire. Maurice snorted at my reaction, but Tam didn't appear to have noticed. After crossing the room, he put several plastic bags down on the table amid the plates. "I was down at the village buying supplies."

"I told you he was running errands," Callum said. "Perry was worried about you."

Thanks for that. "I just wanted to ask if you had a plan. For the mission." I pointedly ignored the vampire's smirk, but Farley's flushed face indicated that she'd picked up on my racing heart too. Just great.

"I figured we could discuss the plan for the mission when we were all awake." Tam scanned our group. "Any ideas?"

"Not exactly, but I looked in our basic files for information on elves." While Tam's expression didn't change, his insistence of Sylvan's innocence earlier came to mind, urging me to tread carefully. "I was curious about the spell on the forest and its cause. There's nothing in the records about elves having any magic, but Maurice says they almost certainly do."

"Don't bring me into your wild theories," said the vampire.

"It's not a theory if it's true," Farley said. "For the record, I agree with Perry. I know none of us like the idea of accusing someone that hunter *wanted* us to blame, but we haven't met many elves before, have we? We don't know what they're capable of."

Tam shook his head. "No, but I have my doubts that Sylvan intentionally put a spell on the forest when he intended to settle peacefully into the village. Like I said, Dylan was trying to steer us in the wrong direction."

"Who else has that kind of magic?" I checked my phone, but Kellen hadn't replied to my message yet. "I can't get internet, but Kellen might be able to get hold of more information from the office…"

"We can't count on him doing so before we leave," said Tam. "Not to rush everyone, but we lost a lot of time yesterday."

"I know. I just wish we had more information." My phone pinged, and I picked it up and saw a reply from Kellen. "What do you mean, classified?"

"Come again?" said Callum.

"Elves." Scowling, I put down my phone. "Kellen said he needed added permission to get access to the files on elves. Bloody higher-ups."

"I expected as much." Was it just me, or did Tam sound almost … relieved? "They can't go handing that information out to everyone."

"They ought to give it to *you*." Disgruntled, I replied to Kellen with a reminder that a child's life was at stake. Whether that would get through to the Wardens was debatable; we'd solved cases on less information than we had now, but that didn't lessen my annoyance.

Kellen didn't reply, however, and my signal flickered on and off while we finished breakfast and went to prepare for our mission.

An hour later, we left the tower. When I pulled out my

wand to cast the transportation spell, Tam held up a hand. "One second."

"What is it?" My stomach flipped. He'd acted normally enough since his return to the tower, but knowing that he hadn't been entirely truthful with me earlier weighed heavily on my mind.

"Can you make sure you picture the village itself as clearly as possible?" he asked. "We don't want to land in the woods again."

"You think we might walk into that spell?" Oh boy. I hadn't even thought of that possibility, but I didn't need to panic and create a self-fulfilling prophecy. "Don't worry, there's less chance of that happening now that I've set foot in the village myself. Everyone ready?"

Maurice answered by disappearing swiftly, heedless of the flicker of worry on Tam's face. My annoyance at the vampire increased tenfold, but I forced my attention to the present, picturing the village clearly in my mind's eye as I waved my wand.

Between one blink and the next, the tower was gone. Someone nearby shouted in alarm, indicating that we'd landed on the central path through the village, in front of an audience of startled villagers. Witches, wizards, and shifters alike goggled at us as if we'd swooped down in a UFO and landed in the middle of their home.

"Oops." I glanced behind me to make sure the others were all there. "I guess that's the problem with picturing the whole village. Nowhere private to land."

"Better than getting lost again," said Callum. "Ah—what's going on over there?"

Recovering from our sudden appearance, the crowd had turned back towards a group of people who thronged the corner of the street where the police station lay. My heart jolted. *Oh boy.*

Tam strode ahead of us, towards the police station. "What's going on?"

A few heads turned our way, including Glenn's. He stood in the doorway. He also appeared to be trying to talk to several people at once and didn't answer Tam when he approached.

"Excuse me?" Tam said to a nearby man, who turned out to be Mr Hutchins.

When Joy's father's spotted our group, his expression became a mask of hostility. "You're too late."

"For what?" My mouth went dry. "Did you find Joy?" *Please say she's alive. Please...*

"No," Mr Hutchins said. "A second child was taken."

8

A *nother child is missing?* I didn't blame Mr Hutchins for being angry with us. We'd not only failed to find Joy, but a second child had joined her overnight, and we were none the wiser.

"I'm sorry to hear that," Tam said to him. "We'd be more than happy to look for the other child as well as your daughter."

"I hope you'll put in more effort today." Mr Hutchins's sour tone grated on my nerves despite my horror at the newest development. *Taken.* He'd said … the same word Tam had used yesterday.

"Where's that hunter?" I asked, before I could think better of it. "Dylan? Isn't he supposed to be helping look for the missing children as well?"

"Him!" Mr Hutchins scoffed. "He hasn't shown his face since yesterday. I bet he's run off."

I wouldn't lie—no longer having to deal with his annoying presence or his attempts to lead us astray wasn't the worst outcome—but I had a feeling we wouldn't get off that easily. Especially if Maurice had run into the hunter on the way to Pleasance Grove.

"Regardless, I'd appreciate it if you could tell me the details," Tam told Mr Hutchins. "Who disappeared? When?"

"A boy from Joy's class called Lloyd Braxton," he said. "His parents said he disappeared before school this morning. He was meant to be in his room, but they said he must have gone outside without them noticing."

"Where do they live?" I asked, already suspecting the answer.

"On our street," he replied. "Two houses down from ours."

Near the same part of the forest. I thought so.

"Is your wife at home?" Tam asked.

"Of course she is," he said. "She's distressed enough without having to witness more panicking parents needing to deal with that imbecile Glenn."

I glanced in the direction of the imbecile in question, but he was too busy staving off questions to notice the insult. "Can we talk to her?"

I didn't know if her Seeing abilities had alerted her to the second disappearance, but I figured Tam wanted to follow up with some questions about the spell on the forest from the previous day. Her husband might have denied all knowledge of the spell, but she might not, and while Glenn was another person we needed to ask about it, we had zero chance of getting near him anytime soon.

"I suppose," said Mr Hutchins, "but I'd prefer for you to get on with the search as quickly as possible. We can't lose anyone else." His anger had faded, replaced with desperation. Something about his attitude still rubbed me the wrong way, but maybe it shouldn't have. He was simply a father desperately worried for his daughter and with no one to place the blame on than the people who'd failed to find her.

"We'll do our best," Tam said. "Shall we go?"

I was happy to leave the crowd behind, and the rest of us followed him as we walked past the stares and whispers. Once we'd escaped, I addressed Mr Hutchins. "Out of interest, why'd you use that word? *Taken?*"

"Is it not accurate?" he asked. "Someone took my Joy, and now they've taken a second child too."

Does he mean a person? I couldn't think of a diplomatic way to ask, so I kept my mouth shut. As we turned into the Hutchinses' street, I slowed my pace, scanning the houses nearby. "This is the place where Lloyd vanished?"

"I guess." Callum eyed the closed curtains of the house two doors down from Mr and Mrs Hutchins. "There isn't anyone in, though. They're at the police station."

"Yeah." I indicated the trees shadowing the houses from behind. "Want to find Maurice first?"

"He can join us later." Callum joined the rest of us as we waited for Mr Hutchins to open the front door. "There are already enough of us here."

"I guess." I dropped my voice. "Do you think he might have run into that spell again?"

"What's that?" Mr Hutchins asked. "Did you say something?"

Not wanting to bring up the spell just yet, I changed course. "I was just asking if Lloyd might have gone into the forest, like Joy did. Did they know one another?"

"They were friends," he said shortly, pushing the door inward. "Clementine? The Wardens are back."

"Are they?" Mrs Hutchins's voice drifted out of the living room. "Do they know about … about…?"

"Lloyd? Yes, they do." He beckoned to us, and I followed the others with reluctance in case my presence set off another reaction from his wife. Since she hadn't freaked out the second time she'd seen me yesterday, I assumed she'd got over the shock, but you never really knew with Seers.

I was the last to enter the living room, and as was typical, I found myself sitting next to the crystal ball again. Mrs Hutchins made a quiet, frightened noise when she saw me, but she didn't scream again or tell us to leave.

"I was sorry to hear about Lloyd," Tam began. "He and your daughter were friends, were they?"

"Yes... Joy was friendly with all the other kids, though. She loved making friends." Mrs Hutchins sniffed. "I wish she was home right now."

"We'll do our best to find them both," Tam said. "Do you know if Lloyd might have intended to go looking for Joy? I gather he left the house when his parents weren't looking."

Good question. Mr Hutchins didn't look pleased at Tam's comment, but his wife sniffed again. "I suppose ... he might have," Mr Hutchins said. "But we won't know until we find them both, will we?"

Tam inclined his head. "I expect not, but it helps to know the details. I understand the police are busy... Do they plan to send anyone into the forest again?"

"I expect so," said Mr Hutchins. "There weren't any witnesses this time."

"That Dylan guy wasn't there?" I queried.

Mrs Hutchins flinched. "The hunter? I don't know... I can't imagine he wouldn't have come forward if he had information."

Would he? The guy was a professional killer, not a finder of missing children. Admittedly, the same applied to our group, but we wouldn't have hidden in the forest if we had pertinent information to share with the police.

"I see," said Tam. "I had one more question... Have you ever met Sylvan?"

"Me?" Mrs Hutchins asked. "No, but Wade has, haven't you?"

"I told you that yesterday." An irritable note entered her

husband's voice. "Are you going to keep asking me the same questions?"

"Sylvan lives in the forest," I cut in, one eye on Mrs Hutchins. "He was also a witness to your daughter's disappearance, and when we went to see him yesterday, he behaved … strangely. Suspiciously."

Tam gave me a warning look that made my heart sink, but I hadn't had a clue how else to broach the subject. Yes, Tam didn't suspect Sylvan himself, but did Mr and Mrs Hutchins?

"Suspicious?" echoed Mr Hutchins. "You think *he* was involved in our Joy's disappearance?"

"Nobody from here would ever take our child," his wife said firmly. "Absolutely not."

"I'm sure you're right," Tam said. "What Perry meant to say was that Sylvan rarely seems to leave the forest. Did you meet him inside the village itself?"

"Where else?" said Mr Hutchins, sounding disgruntled. "Honestly. I'm not convinced you're as professional as you say you are."

"We're monster hunters, not private detectives." I hadn't intended to pick a fight, but I was more insulted on Tam's behalf than on mine. "If you want the police to handle this, ask Glenn. Our job is to find magical monsters and punish them if necessary."

Mrs Hutchins made a choked noise. "Monsters… Did a monster take my Joy?"

"Stop that," her husband said sharply to us. "Now look, you're distressing her again."

Sensing that I was fighting a losing battle here, I rose to my feet to leave. "We don't know what or who took your daughter, but we can't figure out any answers as long as we're in the dark about what's going on in that forest. I have a hard time believing nobody else in the village has noticed the place is covered in a spell that caused us to lose a whole day."

"That's absurd," Mr Hutchins said, his face flushing. "Do you take us for fools?"

I backed towards the door, repelled by his sudden anger. "I'm not lying. It was a spell—"

Callum moved to my side and gave my arm a warning squeeze. "We should go."

Farley whimpered from her seat, while Mr Hutchins got to his feet too. "I didn't expect Wardens like yourselves to come up with absurd excuses to avoid doing your jobs—"

Mrs Hutchins screamed. All eyes snapped over to the Seer, whose head was in her hands as she mewled, rocking back and forth.

Then her head lifted, her eyes wide and haunted. "I see... I see trees, and a path without any end in sight, and ... Joy. My Joy!"

Her husband hastened to her side, alarmed, as she continued rocking, sobbing quietly. I backed out the door, seizing an excuse to get the hell out of there before the situation deteriorated even further. Callum went to help Farley to her feet, while Tam was fast on my heels as I left the Hutchinses' house behind.

A path without end. Trees. She'd seen a vision of the forest, I was sure, but asking for the details would have to wait until later. Assuming Mr Hutchins let us back in the house at all.

"Perry—where are you going?" Tam called as I approached the trees bordering the road. "Don't go back into the forest."

I spun back to him and saw a white-faced Farley collapse against Callum as he closed the door to Mr and Mrs Hutchins's house. "We have to go back in there at some point if we want to find Joy."

"I don't disagree, but it's too dangerous to walk in there without a plan," Tam warned. "We need to find Maurice too."

"Right." I'd forgotten about the vampire. "I bet he's somewhere in there as well."

"And that hunter," added Callum, holding Farley upright. "That vision suggested Joy *was* in the cursed part of the forest, so how do we get her out?"

Tam drew in a breath. "I'll have another look myself, and I'll talk to Sylvan about that spell. Alone."

"You don't want any of us to go with you?" My heart sank again. "I thought you didn't want the team to split up."

"I don't." His attention sharpened; beside us, Maurice had appeared on the road as silently as a ghost. "There you are. Did you see anything in the forest yourself?"

"No, but I saw our hunter friend sniffing around," said the vampire. "Picking up toadstools. I hope he poisoned himself, personally."

Tam inhaled sharply. "That's bad news."

"What, that he's still here?" It was an inconvenience, certainly, but I was confident enough that he knew about the spell on the forest to want to question him on his motives for sending us to Sylvan's house yesterday. "Should we speak to him first?"

Tam exhaled. "I don't think that's a good idea. Not if he intends to lead us astray again."

"He doesn't," Maurice said. "He doesn't think we're coming back at all, in fact."

"You read his mind?" I guessed. "*Did* he know about the spell?"

"If he did, he wasn't thinking about it." Maurice gave me a disgruntled look. "If I'd hung around any longer, he'd have noticed me watching him."

"I thought you were a master of stealth."

He scoffed. "Obviously, but he's trained to hunt people like me."

"Leave the hunter," Tam ordered. "I'll go into the forest myself and speak to Sylvan."

"What—alone?" The vampire shook his head. "Not a chance."

"See?" I gave Tam a pointed look. "Even Maurice thinks it's a bad idea. What if you get stuck for hours again?"

"Or longer?" Callum asked. "Why do you have to go there by yourself?"

"Because one of us is less of a target than a whole group," he replied. "I have a potion that will help me if I run into the same spell as before. It enables me to see through illusions—I got it from the village."

"You did?" Why hadn't he told us earlier? "Do you have enough for more than one person?"

"No." Tam drew a breath. "I'm sorry, everyone, but I need to do this alone. Can you wait for me here?"

"What's got everyone all wound up?" Maurice asked. "The other kid who vanished?"

"You read that from the hunter's mind too?" Evidently, Dylan had figured out that a second child was missing, but he still wasn't exerting himself to find either of them. "Yes, but we spoke to the Seer as well. She had another vision of the woods," I said.

"And Joy." Tam approached the forest entrance. "I won't be long."

How do you know for sure? Panic squeezed my chest, and the urge to follow him rose inside me like a wildfire. Before I'd quite got a grip on myself, I followed him to the forest entrance. "You should take one of us with you. Even two people is better than one, right?"

His gaze swept over me. "Not this time."

The simple phrase pinned me to the spot as he turned

around and walked away, and a riot of confusion brewed in my mind. "Why…?"

"Leave it," Maurice said in a bored voice. "He's committed. Let him go."

I spun back to the others and caught sight of Farley's ashen face. Had she picked up on my tumultuous emotions? "Aren't you worried he'll get stuck again?" I asked.

"If anyone can find their way out of a spell, it's Tam," said the vampire. "He was the one who got us out yesterday in the first place."

"And he had a potion to help, he said," added Callum. "Should we head back to the police station?"

"I doubt that'll help," I muttered. "Glenn's clueless, and he has his hands full dealing with Lloyd's parents already."

"Anyone want to go torment that hunter?" Maurice asked conversationally. "I can take you to him."

"I'm up for it." I looked at the others. "Farley, are you okay?"

She nodded, her breaths shallow. "Remind me never to go into the same room as a Seer again."

"Was it that bad?" I asked.

"Yes, and her husband was as scared as she was." She took in another breath. "You lot weren't helping by panicking either. Especially you, Perry."

"Me?" Heat flooded my face once more. I'd always prided myself on keeping it together … unless she meant my more recent reaction to Tam's departure. I wasn't going there, so I cleared my throat. "Doesn't anyone else think it's a bad sign that our team leader has gone off into a potentially cursed forest alone, after a Seer has had a vision of impending doom?"

"Not really," said Maurice. "He knows what he's doing."

"He didn't even give us instructions." I folded my arms

across my chest, another chill sweeping down my spine. "Why'd he want to talk to Sylvan alone, I wonder?"

"Does he suspect the elf after all?" Maurice said. "It sounded that way."

"I thought not, but … I don't know." Rattled, I faced the vampire. "Did you read anything else from the hunter's thoughts? Or do you want to go back for another round?"

He grinned. "I can get him to spill his guts without needing to poke into his thoughts."

"Please don't," Callum said. "Tam wouldn't like it."

"He's not here," Maurice said. "He never said who got to give the orders in his place either."

That was true, and it was another reason for the worry squirming in my guts. "That hunter guy definitely knows that spell exists. I say we need to find out the extent of his knowledge. What do you think?"

"Tam told us to leave him alone," Callum said.

"Will he leave *Tam* alone?" I asked. "I don't know about you, but I'm not all that keen on the idea of turning our backs on him after what Dylan did to us yesterday."

"I'm with Perry," said Farley, which surprised me. "Come on, Callum, you don't like the hunters any more than the rest of us do. Tam would understand."

"He gave us an order."

It didn't sound like one to me. I didn't need to say so when the others had heard as clearly as I had. In fact, Tam hadn't been acting like our leader at all.

And if I couldn't follow him, I could at least stop the one person in the forest who I knew was both up to no good and within our reach—unlike whoever had taken those children.

A moment passed before Callum sighed. "Okay, I'm outvoted. Let's go."

We made for the forest entrance and let the vampire take the lead. While Maurice affected an exaggerated slow pace so we could keep up, I walked slowly, keeping both eyes on the backs of the houses from which the children had disappeared. The area was so overgrown that an elf might have been hiding in the bushes and I wouldn't have known, but I saw no signs of anyone until Maurice led us to a large oak tree. The hunter crouched nearby, in the process of pulling up a bright-red-spotted toadstool by the roots.

"That's definitely poisonous," I commented. "Conjuring up another way to get rid of us?"

"You." He released the toadstool. "What are you doing here? Here to cause more trouble?"

"No, we've come for answers." I approached Dylan, my caution fleeing, and hoped that Maurice was raiding his thoughts while the hunter's attention was on me. "You know about that spell on the forest, don't you? And you know about Sylvan, the elf. Tell me the truth."

He lifted his chin. "Why would I tell you?"

"Because," said Maurice, baring his fangs, "you don't have a choice."

"I'm armed," the hunter growled, one hand at the belt around his waist. "It might create some annoying paperwork if I stake a Warden, but it's starting to look like it'll be worth the risk."

"As if you'd have a chance at catching me," the vampire said.

"Hang on." I hadn't intended the threats to escalate quite this fast. "Don't go staking or biting anyone just yet. I want to help find those children, and since nobody else is talking, and our team leader just went into the spelled part of the forest alone to talk to Sylvan, you're stuck with the rest of us."

"He went there alone?" The hunter laughed. "In that case, your team leader is dead."

9

I strode over to Dylan almost as quickly as the vampire had. "What do you mean, dead?"

"That spell wasn't cast by a human. Your team leader doesn't have a clue what he's walked into."

You're wrong, I wanted to say, but I wouldn't give him the satisfaction of watching me panic. "If the spell wasn't cast by a human—you mean the elf, don't you? Am I right?"

"Don't bother lying," said the vampire from behind Dylan. "Elves have magic that humans don't. We know that. The question is, how'd you figure it out? Or are you conspiring with him?"

Huh? Maurice thought Dylan was working with Sylvan? Or was he just trying to trip him up and cause his thoughts to give away his motives? I could only assume that the vampire was skimming the hunter's mind as we spoke, but I couldn't tell how much information he'd unearthed.

"Conspiring?" The hunter scoffed. "Do you think the elves would willingly want to spread their secrets to humans?"

"Depends on the human." Callum eyed him with marked

dislike. "The hunters have driven the elves out of enough of their territories for them to want to avoid us, haven't they? You did the same to shifters."

Whoa. The anger in Callum's tone surprised me, though he'd also forgotten all about his initial reluctance to go against Tam's orders. Callum was right, though; the hunters *did* have a reputation for coming down hard on werewolves and other shifters who broke the laws, so the subject was bound to be sore with him.

Maurice bared his teeth at Dylan again. "You were saying? Tell us what you know of the spell."

"I don't have to tell you anything," said the hunter haughtily. "It doesn't matter anyway. Even if you read every single one of my thoughts, you'll never be able to undo a spell that isn't part of the same world you live in."

My mouth opened. "Not in this world?"

"You don't know very much for a Warden, do you?" Dylan tried to step around Maurice, but the vampire blocked each of his movements. "Get away from me, vampire."

He presumably knew Maurice was reading his thoughts, but if it was true that there was no way to undo the spell … *no way*. There had to be one.

"If the elf created the spell, he can undo it," I said. "That's how it works for curses."

The hunter gave a short laugh. "Good luck convincing an elf to do something he doesn't want to."

"Was that what you tried to do?" *Had* the elf cast the spell? He seemed oblivious to its presence, unless his confusion the previous day had all been an act. "Those missing children are trapped within the spell, aren't they? If you have zero intention of trying to help them, why are you even here?"

"What's it to you?" He made another attempt to edge away from the vampire. "If you must know, I'm not going near that spell because I don't have a death wish. Happy?"

"No." Maurice matched the hunter's every movement, preventing him from getting away. "You haven't specified *why* going into that part of the forest risks certain death. We all got out of there unscathed yesterday after your bit of trickery."

"That's right," I added, in total agreement with the vampire for possibly the first time ever. Nothing like a common foe to bring people together. "If you sent us in there on purpose to get us killed, that's a good reason for us to call the Wardens' office. What do you say to that?"

"I wasn't trying to get you killed." He didn't sound cowed, exactly, but he must know not to trifle with the Wardens' higher-ups. "There are all kinds of folks that live in those places that aren't friendly to humans, but I figured they'd leave you alone if you were in a group. Alone, though?"

A shiver ran down my spine. "Tam can handle himself. What do you mean by *those places?*"

He shrugged. "The elves might have a name for them. I don't know, and frankly, I don't care."

Hmm. He might well be telling the truth there. The hunters didn't care to know in depth about paranormals, monsters or otherwise.

"So let me get this straight," said the vampire in a lazy tone. "You spent the past two days traipsing around a forest, but you won't even set foot in the place where you know the missing children are? Were you waiting for us to come and find them for you all along?"

"That's enough from you, vampire," he said. "I've told you more than I should have. Go away."

"You haven't told us who you think took those children," I corrected. "Unless it's Sylvan… *Did* he cast the spell? Or did someone else?"

"Him." Dylan scoffed. "He's clueless."

"What?" He didn't suspect the elf after all? "I thought you said the elves had powerful magic."

"Magic doesn't make up for the lack of intelligence," he said. "As you should know."

"Pity you don't have either," Maurice added.

"What about those legends, though?" I asked as the hunter flushed an angry red. "The ones connecting elves to missing children…"

"Human nonsense," said the hunter. "Convenient, though."

"What the hell does that mean?" said Callum. "You want that elf to get into trouble, is that it? Even if he didn't take the kids?"

"I told you to leave me alone." The hunter lunged, suddenly, a wooden stake in his hand. Maurice leapt away from him, but Dylan didn't try to chase him down. Instead, he grabbed the rucksack from the ground and vanished into the bushes at speed.

"Damn, he's fast." I stared after him. "Is he even human?"

"Hunters tend to have a few advantages even when they're not paranormal," said Callum. "Maurice, are you okay?"

"Yes," he snapped. "He didn't touch me. I hope you got everything you wanted from him, because I'm not going near that stake again."

"What did *you* get from his thoughts?" I asked. "Did he happen to think about who cast the spell, if not Sylvan?"

"No," he said. "But the word 'fairies' came up a few times."

"Fairies. They're related to elves, aren't they?"

"No idea," said Callum. "Have you ever met one before?"

"Once or twice." Like elves, fairies kept to themselves, in my experience.

"I haven't," Farley said. "What do they look like?"

"The two I met were half-human, so I don't know." They'd

resembled regular people, maybe with slightly pointier ears. "They have magic, too, I think…"

I pulled out my phone and opened the Wardens' files again, this time scrolling down in search of 'fairies' instead of 'elves.'

"He might be trying to cover for his own cowardice," said Maurice. "Fairies aren't dangerous. They're tiny creatures with wings."

"Those are pixies." That much I remembered, but when I snagged on the word 'fairies,' the file came up blank. "Weird."

"What's weird?" asked Farley.

"I can't find anything on fairies in here."

"Not that unusual," Callum said, reading over my shoulder. "Like vampires and shifters, fairies are too close to human to be classified as monsters."

"No, but the elves' folder had a few sentences," I said. "The one on fairies is completely empty."

"I bet the higher-ups have that information," Farley said. "That's how it usually is."

"Figures." I searched for pixies next and found a brief description of small, pointy-eared creatures that spoke their own language and flew around scattering glitter everywhere. "Pixies are here, but they're classified as nonthreatening."

"That's no use," Maurice said. "Something bigger than that will have taken those kids."

"You don't say." I looked up from my phone, disgruntled. "I wish I'd asked Kellen to get the files on elves *and* fairies. If they have similar magic, they must be classified under the same umbrella."

I tended to ignore the Wardens' overly complicated classification system and look things up on a need-to-know basis, but I knew that all monsters related to the afterworld were shelved in the same category in the files. Did that rule apply to elves, fairies, pixies, and such?

"That rings a bell," Callum said slowly. "Tam would know. He has the classification system memorised."

I'd thought as much. Ill at ease again, I returned my attention to the entry on pixies. *These small fairies scatter glitter wherever they fly, possibly as a side effect of the magic they can use to hide themselves from sight. This magic is known as glamour.*

"Glamour," I murmured. "And … they can hide themselves from sight?"

"Huh?" said Callum.

"This." I held up my phone to show the others. "Pixies can hide themselves using a kind of magic called glamour…"

"Illusion." Maurice swore so loudly that several birds took flight from a nearby tree. "Dammit. Why didn't I see it sooner?"

"Come again?" I swivelled to the vampire. "Did you read something about that in the hunter's head?"

"Obviously." He stomped across the clearing. "Elves and fairies can make themselves *invisible.* They might be watching us at this very instant."

"What?" On instinct, I spun on my heel, scanning the trees in case invisible elves really were watching us. "Oh— was that how the elf made his house disappear?"

"Of course." Farley gasped. "I don't know much about glamour, but if it can create illusions … doesn't that pretty much describe the spell on the forest? Once you're in there, you can't see the way out."

"No wonder those kids couldn't escape." They might not have been taken by a monster at all. Pixies sounded more like mischievous pranksters than villains, but that didn't explain the hunter's evident fear of the spelled part of the forest. Unless it was the simple aversion to setting foot in a spell that would ensnare him without any way of escape.

Another shiver ran down my spine at the thought that we

were dealing with an invisible enemy. Sylvan might seem harmless, but if the elf hadn't cast the spell … who had?

Closing the file, I texted Kellen despite the lack of any signal. *What do you know about fairies?* Naturally, the message didn't go through, but it was better than not trying. "What now?"

"I don't know," Callum murmured. "If we can't see what we're up against, neither can Tam."

"Tam said he had a potion of some kind," said Maurice. "To help him see."

"Right." I'd momentarily forgotten that he'd been prepared … assuming the potion worked on glamour and not just regular illusion spells. Fairy magic was a literal world away from the type of magic any of us was familiar with.

"He does, but how can he fight something he can't see?" asked Farley, her voice faint. "We shouldn't have let him go in there alone."

"Agreed." My skin crawled at the memory of trying to find our way out of that spell without realising its creator might have been inches away. "Anything could have been watching us in there, and we wouldn't have had any idea."

"Tam can take care of himself," Maurice said. "Stop freaking out."

"Doesn't the idea of an invisible monster bother you?" I queried. "One you can't sink your fangs into?"

"Every monster has its weaknesses," he said. "Unlike that cowardly hunter, I don't run away from things I don't understand."

"Does that mean you want to go and help Tam?" I studied Maurice's determined expression in surprise. "I'm not against the idea… What about you two?"

"We won't be much help if we get caught as well," Farley said doubtfully. "Besides, how are we supposed to find Tam if he's already in the spelled part of the forest?"

"The elf," Callum said. "We know the way to his house, don't we? If Sylvan didn't take those kids, I can't imagine he wants to take the blame, so he'll want to take Tam's advice."

"The elf won't be able to avoid being accused if he keeps hiding away," Maurice remarked. "Anyone could see that this all started when he moved to town."

I raised a brow at him. "You agree with Dylan, do you?"

"No." He scoffed. "I think the hunter's a coward who wants to get the credit for finding those kids without making an effort."

"You aren't wrong." For a wonder—but the hunter was the least of our problems now. He'd said Tam was as good as dead, and while Dylan didn't know the first thing about our team or our leader's capabilities, our enemy's invisible nature gave us little advantage. "If we go to the elf's house and Tam isn't there, what then?"

"Whoever said anything about going to the elf's house?" Maurice said. "He's not the kidnapper."

"Wasn't that where Tam went?" I asked. "If the elf didn't cast the spell, he must know who did, considering it's right outside his house."

"Maybe he doesn't realise it's there," Callum suggested. "He can see through the illusion … through glamour … so he wouldn't get lost."

"He'd notice someone casting a spell on his house, surely," Farley said. "Maurice is kind of right, though… If we get to Sylvan's house and Tam isn't there, we'll end up right back in the same trap we walked into yesterday. Unlike Tam, we don't have any potions."

I wish he'd shared them. "We don't know where the illusion begins or where it ends, but we might be able to find out if we approach the elf's house from a different angle."

"Really?" Callum asked sceptically. "I guess if we keep the

village within sight, we might be able to avoid stepping out of bounds. The closer we are to the village, the safer we are."

"We'd be even safer if we stayed here and waited for Tam like he told us to," Maurice grouched.

"And if he doesn't know what we're up against?" I asked. "We have information that might help us get those kids back. Tam needs to know."

None of the others had any arguments, but Maurice continued to gripe about disobeying orders as we made our way around the village. Even his vampire speed couldn't escape an illusion that stood directly in his path, and for all his bravado about not fearing invisible monsters, he let Callum overtake him as we walked among the tree roots and dodged low-hanging branches.

When my feet sank into an unexpected swamp, I swore. "I can see why the villagers don't take walks in here. Nature is deadly."

"Especially those." Callum indicated a cluster of spotted toadstools like the ones the hunter had been examining earlier.

"Oh yeah." I glanced at the vampire. "Did you read anything in Dylan's mind about why he was so interested in those toadstools?"

"No," he said shortly. "Forget the hunter."

"Okay, then." What had Maurice on edge this time? I was no fan of the swamp, either, nor the thick mud that covered the path and made each step akin to slipping on an ice rink.

We ought to be nearing the elf's house by this point, but when we reached a brook, the vampire's steps came to a sudden stop at the edge.

"What is it?" I tensed. "Did you see someone?"

He gave me a sarcastic look. "Did you leave your brain behind today?"

"Maurice," Callum said, catching up. "What—oh. The water."

"Right, vampires can't cross running water." I'd been too fixated on finding the elf's house and running into a potential illusion to remember that other obstacles might bring us to a halt. Such as vampires' inexplicable aversion to running water. "Is that why you hate puddles so much?"

Maurice gave me a rude gesture, while I looked for a route to cross the river.

"We'll have to walk around that way." Farley pointed. "Which … which means going out of sight of the village."

"Not if one of us waits here," Callum said. "Maurice, if you aren't crossing the river, can you stand somewhere we can see you?"

The vampire pulled a face. "You want to use me as a landmark?"

"You don't want to come with us, do you?" Farley asked. "You can be our lookout."

At least we won't have to listen to any more whining. Why he had such a problem with rivers, I didn't know. The vampires' file was almost as empty as the elves', after all, though vampires' aversion to rivers was handy knowledge to have when one fought them as much as I did.

Leaving the vampire, I followed Callum farther down the river until we found a set of stepping stones. The werewolf reached the other side in one bound, but Farley and I had to balance on the stones to get across. The werewolf's attention was half-fixed on Maurice the whole time, and when we joined Callum on the other side, I followed his gaze to see the vampire pacing irritably up and down the riverbank.

"He does make an effective landmark," I whispered to the others. "But I didn't realise we'd have to leave him behind."

"No." Callum walked a little farther. "Shouldn't we have reached the elf's house by now? It should be over there."

I followed his gaze, but no houses materialised. "How do you know?"

"It smells familiar over here." He trekked through the swamp bordering the river's edge and onward, until we came to a distinct path leading from the houses into a clearing.

"Did we walk past it?" I risked glancing away from the village to scan the area, but it was bare, empty of all signs of habitation. "Has the elf hidden his house again?"

If so, where's Tam? Is he still in there somewhere?

Farley gasped. "Look."

My heart jolted. She'd pointed at an object lying on the ground. At first glance, it appeared to be an ordinary stick, but it was too polished to have fallen from a tree.

It was Tam's weapon.

10

I crouched down and picked up the stick, but no sign of its owner appeared. Neither did the elf's house, though I was certain it ought to be nearby.

"It's gone." My voice sounded small, uncertain. "The elf must have put a glamour on his house … and there's a good chance that wherever he is, Tam's there too."

"But what about that spell?" Callum turned back to the river. "It can't have disappeared, can it?"

"It might have," said Farley. "We don't know where it came from in the first place, do we?"

"The elf knew, even if he wasn't responsible himself." I turned the stick over in my hand, my pulse racing. "He can't have taken Tam, can he?"

No. Tam wouldn't let himself be overcome that easily. He'd overpowered a demon and survived fighting the possessed inspector, for crying out loud. How could a four-foot-tall elf and a magical forest defeat him? Sure, the elf had powerful magic, and anything might be hiding in the spelled part of the woods, and he was unarmed… *That's enough, Perry.* Tam had been prepared to deal with anything, I knew, and the sight of Farley's trembling hands prompted me to try to rein in my fear and focus on the present.

"We can ask the villagers," Callum suggested. "The ones who've met Sylvan might have gone to his house."

I had my doubts that they had, or else there'd have been a lot more reports of people getting lost in the forest. Then again, we hadn't asked anyone but the Hutchins family—not even Glenn.

"Glenn's met him," I recalled. "I doubt that guy would notice a spell if he walked straight into it, though."

"It's somewhere to start." Farley gave a shaky nod. "Ah—where's Maurice?"

I turned back to the river, but the vampire had disappeared. Typical. "Has he gone to threaten the hunter again, I wonder?"

"I thought he wanted to avoid being staked," Callum said. "Nah, he'll have got bored of being, what was it, a landmark?"

"Some use that was in the end." I poked the ground with my foot, silently furious with myself for not following Tam while I'd had the chance.

"There is Mr Hutchins too," Farley pointed out. "If he knows anything, or his wife does… She definitely saw the forest in her vision, didn't she? She might have seen Tam as well."

"And her kid," I added. "I guess we might as well hope that Joy and Tam have found each other … and Lloyd too."

But what about their kidnappers? I didn't voice the last part aloud, but unease clouded our group as we left the path and returned to the village. As before, villagers surrounded the police station, and the stares from people we passed made my temper even more brittle than it was previously.

"Excuse me." I motioned towards Glenn. "I need to talk to the police urgently. Can you move?"

"You're new in town, aren't you?" A young woman I vaguely

recognised as the one we'd asked for directions yesterday stepped into my path. "Where's that handsome friend of yours?"

"You mean Tam?" Her words struck me like a sharp knife, and my hand clenched on the stick I'd brought with me. "He's … in the forest."

"Oh." Her face fell. "I hope he hasn't run into trouble. Some local kids have gone missing in there, do you know?"

"Yes, I'm aware." My patience frayed at the edges. "That's why we're here—to find them. On that note, have you ever met the guy who lives in the forest? Sylvan?"

"Oh, him?" She nodded enthusiastically. "He's very fun."

"Fun?" I repeated. "He moved to town about two weeks ago, didn't he? And he's the only elf in town?"

"The only *what*?" She blinked. "Elves? No, we don't have any of those."

"Sylvan is an elf." Was she really that dense? Or—wait a moment. "What did he look like when you met him?"

"Oh, a little old man, about this high." She measured up to her shoulder with her hand. "He was very kind. He warned me about following the little winged creatures. Said they'd lead me astray."

"What?" I took a step back, tension crawling up my spine. "You've seen a little winged creature?"

"Oh, no, I haven't," she said. "He said I was probably too old for them to come after me but to be careful all the same."

"Perry?" Callum ambled over to my side. "I think we should get out of here… What is it?"

"Elves." Or pixies, rather. *They only show themselves to chil-dren?* If that was the case … we had to talk to Mr and Mrs Hutchins again. "Never mind. Thanks for talking to us."

I left the confused-looking teenager and joined my group, leaving the crowd behind. Whispers tailed us, but I paid them no notice.

"Who was that?" asked Farley. "Why are you so freaked out this time?"

"I think Sylvan has been hiding that he's an elf from the villagers," I whispered to her. "That girl described him as an old man—a human one. It'd explain why Glenn wasn't bothered either."

"Sylvan was using glamour to hide his real appearance?" Callum surmised. "No wonder nobody questioned why an elf moved to the village."

"But is he guilty or not?" asked Farley. "You think he captured those children?"

"No," I said, "but he warned that girl about not following the little winged creatures into the forest. He said she was too old…"

"Too old." Callum stopped in his tracks. "By 'little winged creatures,' he was talking about pixies or something similar, wasn't he?"

"So much for harmless." Chills broke out on my arms. "I think we should talk to Joy's parents again. Even if those creatures are invisible to adults, Mrs Hutchins might have seen another clue in her visions."

Her husband would not be thrilled to see us again, but this time, we did have a genuine update … and Seers could see what ordinary eyes couldn't.

Did that extend to glamour, though?

"Agreed." Callum nodded to Farley. "Are you okay with coming in? Or would you rather wait outside?"

"To find Tam, I'll deal with it," she replied. "Bring it on."

We made a beeline for Mr and Mrs Hutchinses' house. This time, Callum knocked on the door, though once again, Mr Hutchins answered.

"You're back already," he said. "Have you already given up? Where's your team leader?"

"In the forest." I held up the sticklike weapon. "I found this lying outside of the area where he disappeared."

Mr Hutchins's mouth opened. "Disappeared?"

"He wouldn't have dropped this unless he ran into trouble." I lowered my arm, my hand clenching so hard around the stick that it trembled. "He isn't in the forest. He's gone—and so is Sylvan's house. If there's anything you know about him—or about elves and fairies in general, now would be a spectacular time to tell us."

He stared, jaw agape, for a long moment, before I heard Mrs Hutchins's voice from behind him. "Wade?"

He recovered a little. "The Wardens are back... Their team leader is missing in the forest, they say, like Joy is. What do you expect us to do about that? If we knew where Joy was, we wouldn't have needed to ask for your help."

"I know," I said delicately, "but if there's anything you haven't already told us, it might save your daughter's life."

"Let them in, Wade," called his wife. "We have to ... we have to tell them."

They do know something else. I hadn't fully suspected until we'd got here, but I had a hard time believing Mrs Hutchins's vision had been devoid of any clues pointing at the elves or the fairies. No way.

Mr Hutchins's shoulders slumped. "Fine, come in."

We followed Mr Hutchins into the living room, where his wife took up her former position on the sofa. Her eyes were wide, frightened, especially when she saw me approach. This time, I didn't sit next to the crystal ball but remained standing within full sight of her.

"Tell us what you know." I gripped Tam's stick tightly in one hand and tucked my arm behind my back so they wouldn't think I was threatening them. "I'm given to understand that Sylvan has been pretending to be human, but he's actually an elf. Did you know?"

"No … no." Mrs Hutchins gulped. "I never met him, but…"

"But you saw others," Callum ventured. "Elves, or fairies."

Mrs Hutchins gave a shallow nod. "Yes. I didn't tell you because … because they might be watching us."

"Now?" I tensed. "When did you see them? Where?"

"I saw—brief glimpses," she whispered. "They're good at hiding from humans, but I've seen them."

Her husband sat down and put an arm around her. "It distresses her to talk about her visions. Is this relevant?"

"Of course it is," I said. "They aren't just visions. Your daughter was taken by the fairies, wasn't she?"

"That's where we should start," Callum agreed. "Give us the full story."

Mrs Hutchins gulped again. "Joy… She was acting strangely a few days ago. She told me she'd made some new friends in the woods. Little creatures with wings who spoke a strange language."

"She told you that?"

She flinched. "Yes, but you know children… She always had an overactive imagination. Then the other day, she was outside playing alone. I heard her talking to someone, and when I looked, she was playing in the garden with … with *them*."

I pulled out my phone, loaded the image of the pixie, and showed it to her. "Did they look like this?

She jumped violently. "Yes!"

"What is that?" her husband asked.

"A pixie." I showed him. "We don't have that much information on them, but the file says they're harmless."

It also said they liked to play tricks on humans, though. Had they lured Joy into a trap laid by a more dangerous fairy?

"Harmless?" Mr Hutchins growled. "Why'd they take her, then?"

His wife sobbed. "I was scared for her, and I told her not to play with them any longer. Maybe that was why they took her."

"They probably lured her into the forest," I guessed. "But I don't know why. And—if Sylvan was nearby, why didn't he stop them?"

Mrs Hutchins sobbed again. "I don't know. Sylvan and I have never met. Is he really … not human?"

"That doesn't mean he took her," Callum said hastily, "but he might have seen who did. The problem is, when we went to see him yesterday, we walked into a spell."

"Spell?" echoed Mr Hutchins. "He put a spell on you?"

"No, but someone put a spell on the part of the forest where he lived," I said. "It was an illusion, like the ones the fairies use to hide themselves, except they hid an entire section of the forest, and from the inside, it was impossible to see the way out. That was how we got lost. I was telling the truth."

"And they took my Joy there?" Mrs Hutchins buried her head in her hands. "I should have known not to trust those winged creatures."

"How much did you tell the police initially?" I asked. "The hunter knows about the fairies. Did you tell him too?"

"No," she whispered. "No … only my husband and Glenn. I asked him to tell Lloyd's parents, but they…"

"They didn't believe us either," said Mr Hutchins, his mouth turning down at the corners. "As you might expect. If Clementine's visions weren't always accurate, I never would have thought such creatures might be hidden inside our village. And if this Sylvan has been deceiving us, he has a lot to answer for."

Unease twisted inside me. While I didn't blame him for

reacting that way to the deception, I didn't believe Sylvan was the kidnapper either. And I didn't want the hunter to have any more excuses to cause trouble for the villagers. "Sylvan ... I think he's a bit out of it, but he's not the one who took her. We ran into a teenage girl earlier who said that Sylvan warned her not to go into the forest alone."

"He knew?" Anger flickered across Mr Hutchins's face. "Why not warn us too?"

"Maybe he didn't know there were other fairies in the forest until she went missing," Callum suggested. "As I said, we'll talk to him again, but to do that, we'll need to find him. Did you see anything else in the vision you had yesterday? Any landmarks to show what part of the forest Joy was in?"

Mrs Hutchins shook her head. "I wish I knew more, but I only saw brightness and ... and her, alone on a path."

Bright. Magic ... or glamour. *Dammit, there's got to be another way to reach them.*

"That's all we know," Mr Hutchins added. "Are you going to find her now? You aren't leaving the village again?"

"Not when our team leader's missing too," I said. "Trust me, we aren't leaving until we've stopped this and made sure nobody else is taken."

Gratitude flickered across Mrs Hutchins's face, though her husband still looked sceptical. "How do you expect to manage that without your leader?" he asked.

"Now we know what to look for, we have somewhere to start." I might not have a full plan yet, but I had some ideas. "Hunting magical monsters is our speciality. We just need to know their weaknesses."

I did my best to inject confidence into my voice, but the others doubtless saw right through me, especially Farley.

"Thanks for telling us." Callum rose to his feet. "We'll come back if we have more news."

"Yeah." I made the mistake of glancing at the crystal ball

on my way out, which dazzled me with a vibrant light that conjured up spots before my eyes. Blinking to clear my vision, I walked outside, wondering if any other adults in town had abilities like Mrs Hutchins's but kept quiet for fear of being disbelieved or dismissed.

"I think they told the truth," Farley murmured as Callum closed the door behind us. "Based on what I felt from them, they weren't hiding anything this time."

"I was thinking the same," I said. "The problem is that these pixies seem to only show their faces to children. I don't think any of the locals would be thrilled if we kidnapped their kids to use as bait."

"Definitely not," said Callum. "We don't necessarily need bait, though, not if we can find our own way into their realm."

"True, but Perry's reminded me that we don't know their weaknesses," said Farley. "The fairies are bound to have at least one, aren't they?"

"Dylan would know," I said. "Should we find him again, do you think? We'd need Maurice to read his thoughts, though, wherever he is."

"He'll be back," Callum said. "You know what Maurice is like. He has no patience for sitting and talking."

"He's still as vulnerable to walking into the fairies' trap as the rest of us are," I said. Even Tam, as it turned out. "Unless he's gone to force Dylan to show us the way to find Sylvan's house."

"Might have." Callum took a few steps towards the forest entrance. "Nah, we'd hear them fighting. Besides, Dylan can't see the fairies any more than the rest of us can, so he won't be much help."

"Who else can we ask?" I thought back to the teenage girl. *Hmm.* "Does the fairies' magic have a cut-off point, do you think? I mean, would someone who was barely a child count?"

"You think one of us should pretend to be under eighteen?" Farley shrank back into her hooded coat and hunched her shoulders. "I could give it a go. I still get asked for ID whenever I buy alcohol."

"Maurice looks younger than the rest of us," I recalled. "But I don't know that the fairies will try kidnapping a vampire either."

"I think they want younger than teenagers," Callum said, shuddering. "If what Sylvan told that girl is anything to go by."

"I was thinking of that too," I said. "She's what, sixteen or so? I feel like if I said Tam wanted to talk to her, she'd happily walk straight into the forest without asking any questions."

"Why would she do that?" Callum asked blankly.

"She has a crush on Tam, I think." Irritatingly, my own face heated at the word 'crush.' "She was disappointed when I said he wasn't around. Anyway, it was just an idea. I don't think any parents want us borrowing their kids to find our way into fairyland either."

"Definitely not," Farley said. "Though teenagers do stupid things without needing encouragement."

That was true, but if Sylvan's words were accurate, the fairies had looked for children to capture, not almost-adults. "If you ask me, we should probably pass on all this information to the police. I know it's probably obvious that the other children in the village might be in danger, but Glenn is dense enough that he might need another reminder."

"That's true," said Callum. "We can pass on what Mrs Hutchins told us, too, for all the good that'll do."

"Worth a shot." The dopey head of the police probably wouldn't be much help, but we had to try every avenue possible.

Without a doubt, the fairies—if they were indeed what we were dealing with—had crossed a line. Did they find it amusing to mess around with humans who couldn't even see them, even going as far as to steal their children? They might not be the conventional monsters we usually dealt with, but I was all too happy to dispense some punishment towards them.

And for taking Tam, I'll make them pay.

11

The crowd outside the police station had dispersed somewhat, but we attracted the usual stares from everyone on the streets when we walked back in that direction. The door was closed, so I could only assume that the parents of the unlucky missing second child had gone home, leaving Glenn to escape to safety.

Not for long. I walked straight to the police station and pushed open the door without knocking. Glenn startled upright from his position on the sofa when I marched in. "Ah—you! The Wardens!"

"That's us." I waited for Callum and Farley to catch up to me, figuring that the vampire would keep his distance as usual. "We'd like to ask you some questions."

His mouth parted. "About Lloyd Braxton? The second missing child?"

"No," I said. "About the kidnappers. The fairies."

His mouth dropped open. "What?"

The panic in his eyes wasn't lost on me. "Dylan told you, didn't he? He told you there were fairies in the forest and that they were responsible for capturing the children. Now they've also taken our team leader, so it's personal."

His eyes bulged, and he fell backwards against the sofa cushions. "What? You lost your team leader?"

"Pull yourself together," I snapped. "We didn't lose our team leader. He went into the forest to look for the two missing children. If it turns out you knew and didn't warn us—"

"I don't!" he yelped. "I don't know who took those kids."

"But you do know the fairies were involved?" Callum asked. "Dylan mentioned something to you, didn't he?"

"He's the expert," Glenn mumbled. "I don't know anything about—about fairies. Or whatever they are."

When he didn't meet my eyes, my suspicions multiplied. "He's certainly not an expert. You must know that we have a better chance of finding those kids than he does. He told us himself that he has no intention of actively searching for them."

His shoulders slumped. "What do you want from me? I can't order the hunter to leave town."

"I want you to tell us everything he told you about the fairies," I said. "In fact—did Joy's parents mention to you that she was seeing winged creatures in the garden? That she followed them into the forest?"

"Children have wild imaginations," he said uncertainly.

"It wasn't her imagination. Now the same has happened to Lloyd," I said heatedly. "The fairies are hiding themselves from the village's adults, but children can see them, and every single child in this village is in danger until we find the one responsible."

"You have to warn their parents," Callum added. "Have any of them gone looking? Or did you tell them to avoid the forest altogether?"

"No," Glenn said. "Some of the parents did offer to search

the area, but they haven't found anything. Are these … these fairies really invisible to adults?"

"Yes, unless they want to be found," I told him. "And on that note, I think *everyone* should stay out of the forest until we figure this one out. Thanks to the fairies' magic, there's no way for anyone to tell if they're walking into a trap until it's too late."

He paled. "What do you mean?"

"The part of the forest the fairies are hiding in is concealed by a spell," I clarified. "Sylvan's house too."

"Who?" He blinked. "Is that old man involved in this? I haven't seen him today…"

"Yes and no." I didn't want to get someone innocent in trouble, but if Sylvan didn't want to take the blame by default, he might have to reveal his real identity to the other villagers. "He's an elf. He's been disguising himself as a human using magic."

Glenn's brow furrowed. "He looked like an old man to me."

"That's the point." Honestly. How dense could he be? "He also knows who took the children."

Glenn rose to his feet. "Then someone has to find him!"

"Do you know where he lives?" Callum asked dubiously. "Because the part of the forest where he lives has completely vanished, along with our team leader."

"Oh, your leader's with Sylvan?" Some of Glenn's panic faded. "He's not missing, then, is he?"

"Didn't you hear the part where Callum said the elf's house has vanished?" My jaw twitched in annoyance. "I don't know for sure if the children are in the same place, but like I've said—we can't find our way in. The fairies' part of the woods is hidden by glamour."

"You know that word, don't you?" asked Farley, who'd

been quiet until now, no doubt because of the tumult of emotions bouncing among us all. "Dylan told you."

"I don't know how it works," Glenn mumbled. "Glamour, I mean. It's all very confusing."

"Glamour is illusion," I said impatiently. "Only elves and fairies can see through it—and children. Those two kids were lured into the forest and taken somewhere that nobody else can see."

"Dylan confirmed everything," added Callum. "What else did he tell you, Glenn? Did he mention that he had no intention of putting himself in danger to find those kids?"

"I … no." His panicked expression returned. "Of course not. I called the hunters because they were known for getting things done."

"That's one way of putting it." Contempt filled my voice. "They hit first and ask questions later."

"A kid was in danger!" Glenn's voice turned high pitched. "What was I supposed to do? Call the police from the big city? They'd take a week to get here. And—I thought your people would take a week to get through the paperwork too."

Usually they would. Somehow Mrs Hutchins had bypassed that when she'd called the Wardens herself.

"You thought wrong," I said. "Dylan is only in this for himself. Did he mention what his plan was?"

"He…" He hesitated. "He mentioned laying a trap for them. The fairies."

He does have a plan? "What kind of trap?"

Glenn gave a frantic shake of his head. "He didn't tell me the details."

"He must have given something away." I thought back to our own conversations with Dylan and the thoughts Maurice had teased out of his mind. "Everything has its weakness. Even the fairies. Do you know what theirs is?"

"I … I … iron."

"Come again?" I said blankly.

"Iron." He nodded enthusiastically. "Dylan told me that was what fairies were scared of. They can't even touch it."

"What, like steel?" I reached for the knives I kept at my belt, and he recoiled. "Relax, I'm not going to stab you. We're monster hunters, too, remember?"

"Steel is an iron alloy," Farley ventured. "That means your knives ought to work."

"Fairies don't need to be allergic to iron to dislike being stabbed," I added. "So there's that too."

"Carrying iron won't help us actually find the fairies' hiding place, will it?" asked Callum. "The opposite, if anything, if they're afraid to even touch the stuff."

Yeah ... but at least we have a tool to fight them with. "Yes, so it would help if we had a way to see through their illusions."

"You can't," said Glenn. "None of us can. Except..."

"Except the children." That was the crux of the issue. "You did warn all the local parents to keep their children under close watch, didn't you?"

"I—tried," he mumbled. "I'm sure they will. They won't want anyone else to be taken."

Meaning nobody listened to you. "I should hope not."

My phone buzzed in my pocket, and I jumped violently. Someone was calling me.

"What—?" Glenn's exclamation cut off as I ran out of the room, grabbing my phone on the way.

"You got a signal?" Farley hurried after me.

I nodded and answered the call. "Kellen, we have a crisis."

"Oh no." The background rang with static, but it was such a relief to hear my mentor's voice that I didn't care. "Listen— I can't give you access to the files on fairies. You'll have to get Tam to call the office."

"He's *missing,*" I said through clenched teeth. "The fairies captured him."

I waited for my words to sink in as I walked out into the street, leaving the police station in the dust.

"What?" Kellen's raspy voice took on a wary note. "You're … you're not joking, are you?"

"Of course not," I hissed. "Tam told us all to stay behind while he went to question a local elf, and now they've both disappeared. The elf's house was hidden by glamour, but—"

"You know about glamour?"

"I did read the files." I waited for Callum and Farley to catch up with me, paying no heed to the curious locals who glanced after us. "Two kids have been captured by the fairies, and now our team leader has vanished along with the main suspect."

"Suspect?" he echoed. "You think this elf is the kidnapper?"

"No, but he's the only person who has any information on who *is* taking the children." I lowered my voice in case any of the villagers had figured out what I was talking about. "Oh, and there's a hunter in town making trouble as well."

"A hunter?" I heard Kellen swear under his breath as I strode onward. "Listen—I'll try to get through to the higher-ups, but they'll want to talk to Tam, and I don't know that I can persuade them otherwise."

"Surely there's a procedure for 'team leader goes missing in fairyland.'" My hand clenched around the phone. "Can't you tell them that?"

"If you want me to tell them it's an emergency, I can do that," he said. "But their response would be to send in another team—assuming we can find someone who has experience with the fairies and is available right this instant. Which isn't a lot of people. I expect that was why the hunters got involved first."

"No," I cut in. "We don't need to fill the whole village with Wardens who can't see through glamour. If anything, we need fewer people—so if you have anyone who can get rid of the hunter, I'd be glad of it."

"I doubt we can." I heard him riffling through the desk drawers in the background, while Callum and Farley whispered to one another behind me. "Especially if he got there first," Kellen continued. "Which branch? Do you know?"

"I didn't ask," I admitted. "We didn't exactly have much in the way of civilised conversation."

"Really, Perry," he said. "You didn't get into a fight with him, did you?"

"I never laid a finger on him." Technically, it was true. "He pretty much admitted he was here to take credit for finding those kids without lifting a finger. I don't know if he expects the fairies to surrender to him of their own accord, but he's refusing to search for the children. The police said he was setting a trap."

"Be careful with him," he warned. "The hunters aren't known for caring who else gets in the way of their goals."

"Believe me, I know." Like most Wardens with any principles to speak of, Kellen viewed hunters' methods with contempt. "The local police—who are useless, by the way— called him in and won't send him packing, but I gather that it doesn't matter to the hunters whether the children are found or not. Two of them have been taken now, and since nobody else can see the fairies, no one can find them."

Kellen sucked in a breath. "Why did Tam go to find them alone?"

"He had something … some kind of potion he said would enable him to see through the illusions and find his way out," I explained. "He was going to talk to the elf, since Sylvan was the only local with the ability to see through glamour. We followed him after we found out the truth, but the elf's house had vanished. We can't get in."

"Elves can be pranksters, but kidnapping people isn't

usually their style," he said. "Maybe Tam is working with him to find the children."

"I've thought so, but if he's run into trouble, we can't do anything to help," I said. "He also left his weapon behind. He never does that."

"No." Kellen was silent for a moment. "I might not be able to give you the files in good time, but I can tell you what *I* know about fairies. Will that do?"

"Of course." I walked to the street's end, where the village merged with the forest, and did my best not to look in the direction where the elf's house was supposed to be. "What do you know about the fairies' magical abilities? Aside from glamour?"

"Glamour is by far the most powerful skill they have at their command," he said. "Their ability to weave illusions is nearly limitless, I'm told. They can make themselves look like anyone or anything, but it sounds like you're dealing with the other side of their glamour … the ability to create pockets of reality in their own design."

Chills raced down my arms again. "Yeah … that sounds about right. Yesterday we got lost in the woods for less than an hour, but we came out to find a whole day had passed."

"It's not uncommon for the fairies' magic to have that effect," he said. "It even shows up in folktales told by normals."

My stomach dropped. "Yeah … about that. The stories also mention elves and fairies capturing human children. Are those stories accurate too? I thought the normals' tales of the magical world were wildly exaggerated."

"They usually are," he replied. "If the fairies *did* take two human children captive, they must have had a reason."

"Whatever the reason, the villagers are panicking," I said. "And Sylvan—the elf—isn't exactly helping. He did warn a few people not to go into the forest, but he seemed surprised to learn that the children's parents would have been worried about them."

"Yes ... elves don't exactly see things in the same way humans do."

"I figured as much," I said. "Also, he's been using an illusion to make most people think he's human, so I can only imagine how the villagers will react when they find out the truth."

"I can see why he's lying low, in that case." I heard the scratching of pen on paper. "I do recall there being ways to pinpoint entrances to the fairies' realm. There are indicators, like circles of toadstools, oddly placed rocks, that kind of thing."

"Toadstools." The word pinged in my mind. "They're all over the forest."

"Sometimes the fairies arrange toadstools in a precise circle, which is called a fairy ring," Kellen said. "If a human steps into that circle, they're transported into the fairies' home."

"A circle?" Wait. The hunter had been picking them up. Had *he* known? "We may have knocked some of those toadstools over when we arrived in the forest ... and the hunter was messing with them too."

"Was he?" said Kellen. "A hunter ought to know better than to purposely damage the fairies' property."

"Damage?" Had Dylan known he might be dismantling an entrance into the fairies' world when he'd picked up those toadstools? "Then—if the toadstools are moved or knocked over, is the way to the fairies' realm closed?"

"Yes, until they open another one," he replied. "I imagine moving the toadstools would only anger the fairies rather than keeping them out of the forest altogether."

"I doubt the hunter cared." We needed to talk to him

again, assuming he'd admit to any wrongdoing. "What happens if he's cut off all the routes in?"

If there'd been a circle—a fairy ring—around the elf's house, had Dylan dismantled that too? Was that why the house had disappeared?

"Like I said, the fairies wouldn't let a human get away with messing with their property," he said. "If anything, you're better off letting the fairies exact revenge upon the hunter themselves."

An appealing prospect … except for one detail. "That won't help us find Tam."

"Look for more toadstools, then. That's all the advice I can give."

"And—what about finding our way out afterwards?" I studied the forest entrance, where Callum and Farley waited in the shadow of a large oak. "Can we use toadstools to get out too?"

"No—that's the issue," he said. "There isn't an equivalent to point you back to the human world. Not one that's visible to human eyes, anyway."

"Tam managed to find the way out the last time," I recalled. "We walked around until he saw a path that looked familiar."

"He must have sharp eyesight," he said. "I expect that was why he volunteered to go back alone."

"That, and he bought supplies to enable him to see through glamour."

"Yes… I've never heard of a potion with those capabilities, at least not one that can be bought on short notice," he said. "Tam knows what he's doing, though."

"Yeah, but the last time we went into the elf's part of the woods, we lost almost a whole day," I said. "I don't know if time is passing differently for the missing children, too, but

Tam might be gone for hours, and I don't know if I'll be able to call you again."

"I know," he said. "I'll do my best to get those files, but I've given you all the information I have. Are you sure you don't want me to send backup?"

"Unless you have a fairy working for the Wardens, or someone who looks like a convincing small child…" I trailed off, seeing a figure emerge from among the trees. The vampire was back. "We'll figure it out. Talk to you later."

"Good luck."

As the call ended, I strode to join my group. Everyone looked at me expectantly, even Maurice.

"What did Kellen have to say?" asked Callum. "What's the plan?"

I surveyed everyone, and my gaze lingered on the vampire. "Let's find that hunter. I think he deserves another prodding, don't you?"

12

"You want to find that guy again?" Farley asked with a grimace. "Why? I thought Maurice already pried everything useful from his thoughts."

"I wouldn't object to another round," the vampire said. "He's still in the forest, not far from where we saw him last."

"You were watching him?" I asked. "He didn't notice you?"

"No, he was too busy picking up those toadstools. God only knows why."

"More of them?" I swore. "Those aren't just toadstools."

"Come again?" Maurice said. "They looked like toadstools to me."

"They belong to the fairies." I drew in a breath. "Kellen told me that circles of toadstools were called fairy rings. They're portals into the fairy realm."

The vampire hissed between his teeth. "Sneaky. I didn't read that in his thoughts."

"Why's the hunter messing with the fairies' property?" asked Callum. "Seems like a good way to get himself into trouble."

"Oh yeah, the fairies won't be happy if they catch him at

it," I added. "I don't know if he realises that or if he just doesn't care, but it's not good news if he's dismantling all the entrances into their world."

"Was that why we couldn't find the elf's house?" asked Farley. "I didn't see any toadstools … though I wasn't looking for them either."

"That's the point. They're hidden in plain sight." I pressed a hand to my forehead. "The question is, has the hunter left any of them untouched?"

"Not if he doesn't want to find those kids." Uncharacteristic contempt dripped from Callum's voice. "I can't believe he's going as far as to make sure nobody else does either."

"How does he expect the fairies to walk into his trap if they can't get out?" Maurice snorted. "Not smart of him."

"Kellen told me the fairy rings were one-way," I said. "I'm guessing the fairies have even more ways to get in and out of their home that they don't share with the rest of us."

"We found our own way out, with Tam's help," said Callum. "I wonder if he knew the trick with the toadstools to get back in?"

"He might have." If so, why hadn't he told us? Did he think we'd have followed? *Well... I might have, but who can blame me?*

A moment's unease passed among our group as we took in the implication of our team leader hiding critical information from the rest of us. Tam knew we were all competent at dealing with monsters, didn't he? Sure, we had never faced up against fairies before, but they could hardly be worse than demons, and we'd dealt with those twice in the short time we'd been a team.

"Dylan's just over there." Maurice pointed towards the forest. "If you want him to put those toadstools back, I'd be happy to shake him until he does."

"Would that work?" Callum asked. "Putting the toadstools back, I mean?"

"Kellen suggested that moving the toadstools or knocking them over stopped the fairy ring from working." That was no doubt one of the reasons the hunter was so committed to taking them apart, even if it prevented anyone else from going to rescue the children too.

"Would those fairy rings work on just anyone?" asked Farley. "Or are they only for children?"

"No, I don't think so," I said. "We already got in there once, if there were toadstools all around that elf's house, and anyone else might have done the same."

Farley's brow scrunched up. "The children were caught because the fairies lured them into stepping into the circles of toadstools. Do I have that right?"

"Yes, and that reminds me." I turned on my heel. "If we found one of the fairies, we might be able to follow them too."

"Where're we going to find one of them, genius?" Maurice said. "If they're hiding from adults, they won't make an exception for us."

"You think there might be more of them hiding among the villagers?" Callum asked dubiously. "Like Sylvan?"

"There might." If there *were* any fairies hidden in the village, it was a safer bet than borrowing someone's child or pretending to be children ourselves ... but that was assuming the fairies would show their faces to us. "They can use glamour to pretend to be anyone."

"Like demons," said the vampire.

"Except the fairies aren't possessing the real person," I added. "But we'd need someone who could see through glamour to identify them in the first place..."

That brought us straight back to square one.

"I don't know. They sound pretty similar to me," said

Maurice. "Both fairies and demons live in a world apart from this one, and they both like screwing around with humans."

"Pity there isn't a fairy equivalent to a summoning circle." Who knew, there might be, but we couldn't wait for the Wardens to permit us to access the extent of their information on fairies. No, our quickest route to finding our way into the fairies' world was to confront the hunter. "Never mind. Let's find Dylan and see what else we can get from him."

The vampire moved into the lead, while I checked my weapons were within reach. If what Glenn had said was accurate, anything made of iron would scare off the fairies, which wouldn't help us *find* them, but it might help me to get Tam away—once I'd put a stop to Dylan's attempts to dismantle every entrance to their realm.

We found Dylan near the elf's clearing—or where it used to be—with his rucksack sitting on the ground next to him. I was willing to bet that if I opened the bag, I'd find a whole stack of stolen toadstools he'd pilfered from the fairies. I didn't bother with stealth, marching straight through the undergrowth towards his spot.

The hunter's eyes narrowed in annoyance. "You again?"

"I know what you're doing." I halted a few feet away from him. "Did you think taking away any access to the fairies' realm would stop them from capturing any more children? Or did you not care?"

"How—?" He broke off, anger colouring his face. "That coward Glenn blabbed to you, didn't he?"

"Actually, our supervisor told us you were dismantling those fairy rings to stop people from using them." Callum came up to my side. "Does *your* supervisor know you're actively endangering those kids by taking away any chance of anyone finding them?"

"I'm not endangering them," he argued. "In fact, I'm stopping any more kids from wandering into the fairies' traps."

"Doesn't seem like you're doing much to find the ones who the fairies have already taken," I said. "How do you expect the fairies to react to you stealing their toadstools?"

"Yeah, that might come back to hit you." Maurice appeared behind the hunter, who reached for the stake at his belt. "Relax, I'm not going to bite you. I'll leave you for the fairies instead."

The hunter's jaw twitched, though I detected a flicker of worry in his eyes that he quickly blinked away. "The fairies can't harm me."

"Because you're carrying iron?" No wonder he was so heavily armed. "That won't stop them, but they might forgive you if you put the toadstools back."

"A likely story," he growled. "You're trying to trick me, aren't you?"

"Actually, we're doing you a favour." Maurice extended a hand towards the rucksack, which the hunter snatched out of reach. As he lifted the bag, I could have sworn it emitted a disgruntled squeaking noise. *Is that the toadstools?*

"What?" said the hunter. "What're you looking at."

"Your bag is squeaking." Glittering, too, if I tilted my head to the side. "Maybe the fairies are already enacting their revenge on you."

"They aren't," he said. "Like I said, I have iron, and I'm not afraid to use it."

"Who are you threatening?" I dragged my gaze from the rucksack. "Do you think the fairies are watching you at this very instant?"

They might have been, in fact. Pity we couldn't use this guy as bait. They weren't interested in capturing adults ... though they might make an exception for someone who really ticked them off. *Hmm.*

Maurice bared his teeth in a grin. "Sure, they are."

Seeing the hunter's growing unease, I pressed my advantage. "Those toadstools might be one way into the fairies' realm, but they aren't the only method."

The hunter made a sceptical noise. "Says who?"

"You know they might be watching." I gestured to the clearing. "The fairies' realm might be separate from ours, but it's here whether we can see it or not. Stealing the toadstools won't stop them."

"Your point?"

"The elf's house was right there, as you know well." Despite myself, I squinted in that direction as if trying to see through tinted glass, but my human eyes weren't good enough.

Another squeaking noise drew my eyes back to the hunter's bag, which he'd placed down at his side. When the bag rocked sideways, I peered more closely. "Is that ... moving?"

The hunter stepped in the way. "When will you give up and get out of here? The fairies aren't going to answer you."

"Fairies." Callum narrowed his eyes. "What *is* in that bag? It's moving."

So it was. Maurice edged around behind Dylan, trying to get closer, but the hunter drew a wooden stake.

The bag continued to twitch, shedding more glitter, and something tickled at the edges of my memory. The children had been lured into the forest by a small, winged creature...

I lifted my head sharply. "That's not a toadstool, is it?"

"It's alive?" Farley looked aghast. "You didn't capture one of the fairies, did you?"

"Don't be absurd," Dylan snarled, but he couldn't disguise that the bag was vibrating as if it might sprout wings and take off at any instant. "Can't you mind your own business?"

"I'm pretty sure there's a law against capturing magical

creatures without a licence." I reached for my phone, though as I'd predicted, the signal had disappeared again. "Should I check with your bosses?"

"I think they'll be pleased that I stopped the creatures from stealing any more children." The shifty look in his eyes betrayed his displeasure at getting caught in the act. "You're bluffing."

"What was the point in catching a fairy?" asked Callum. "Did you plan to ask it to show *you* the way in?"

"Maybe."

I had my doubts. Dylan had clearly had no intention of putting his own life in danger, but his captive *did* undeniably know the way into the fairies' realm. And if we set the creature free, it might lead us to Tam *and* the missing children. I caught the vampire's eye, hoping he'd be willing to help, but he shook his head. Evidently, he didn't want to step within range of the hunter's stake, but the rest of us didn't have a vampire's advantage of speed.

I turned my attention towards Callum instead. If the werewolf shifted, he might be able to take the hunter by surprise, but the hunters were well known for carrying weapons that could take down a shifter, and he was no doubt prepared for us to jump at him.

No … we needed a distraction. We had the guy outnumbered, at least, so we had that going for us.

Here goes. I pulled out my wand first to draw his attention. "You might have iron, but you can't defend yourself against this."

"I'm not afraid of magic." Dylan fixed his gaze on me, but he kept the stake in his hand, preventing the vampire from reaching the bag at his feet. It continued to rock back and forth, emitting distinct squeaking sounds.

I took aim but not at the hunter. Instead, my spell crashed into a tree, causing leaves to shower down on the clearing.

The vampire darted behind Dylan, but the hunter wasn't fooled.

"Give it up." He spun on his heel, gripping the stake. "You're wrong if you think I won't stake a Warden."

He lunged, and as Maurice sprang out of range, I gave another flick of my wand, this time aiming at Dylan's feet. Leaves showered upward, and the bag tumbled over onto its side.

At once, a winged creature shot out of the open rucksack and streaked across the path like a bullet. I glimpsed pointed ears and glitter trailing from beating wings, and the hunter swore explosively when he saw his captive escaping.

"Wait!" I broke into a sprint, following the trail of glitter as I fought to keep the pixie within sight. "Hey! I need to find my friend. Can you lead me to your home? I know I'm not a child, but … you probably don't understand a word I'm saying, do you?"

I heard the hunter shambling around and cursing behind me, but I didn't dare take my eyes off the pixie, not even to blink. Despite my knowledge that the creature had intentionally led a couple of children into a dangerous realm, the pixie's obvious terror and the cruel way the hunter had treated it brought an unexpected surge of pity for the small creature.

"I'm not going to hurt you," I called out. "I just want to find those children."

The pixie turned back, eyes wide and frightened—then it disappeared.

"No." Heart sinking, I ran up to the spot where the pixie had vanished, hands raised to catch the glitter as if I could make it reappear by sheer force of will. "I know you're still there. Help—"

I broke off when a pink haze smothered the world, and I blinked furiously, trying to clear my eyes. The hunter's shouts had faded to silence, and I couldn't hear my team-mates either. I *could* hear the pixie, its faint chittering coming back into focus like the volume being turned up.

When I opened my eyes properly, the first thing I saw was the elf's house, sitting a few feet away. *Was this where it vanished to? Then...*

I ran towards the house, where the door lay open. Sylvan peered out, and next to him—

"Tam." My knees went weak with relief at the sight of him standing outside the house, unharmed and unchanged. "Hey —Tam!"

When Tam turned towards me, his expression filled with horror. "Perry? No ... you shouldn't be here."

"What?" Maybe it was the disorientation from my sudden trip across realms, but for some reason, his words didn't sink in for several seconds. I'd already pulled out the sticklike weapon he'd left behind when it hit me that he didn't look happy to see me in the least.

The elf, meanwhile, eyed me with mild surprise. "Oh, hello. I wondered if I'd see you again."

"Sylvan." I forgot everything I planned to say, since I needed to know why Tam was looking at me like I'd single-handedly doomed us all. "Tam. I thought you'd gone. The house disappeared, and I didn't know if you'd be able to find your way back. Are you okay?"

Sylvan squinted at me. "How extraordinary. You're human. How did you find your way here?"

"I followed the pixie." I gestured upward as the little crea-ture flew overhead, squeaking loudly. "The hunter captured him. Dylan did. I think he wanted to stop anyone from rescuing those children—are they here?"

"Perry..." Tam trailed off. "No, they aren't here."

"Then why...?" The accusation and anger in his expres-sion scrambled my thoughts. I'd almost rather he hadn't been looking at me at all. "What have you been doing all this time?"

"All this...?" His eyes widened in understanding. "How long has it been? I did tell you to wait for me, didn't I?"

"Yes." My face flushed. "Yes, and it hasn't been *that* long, but we thought you were in danger. We found out that the fairies were using glamour to trick people, including him."

I glared at Sylvan, who blinked. "Excuse me?" he asked.

"You were disguising yourself as a human." Why was Tam still looking at me as if I'd committed a crime? I was telling the truth. Surely he knew that. "The other villagers had no idea you were an elf, so they were completely unprepared for the fairies to start capturing them."

"I was telling him that the villagers were worried for their children," Tam said, before turning back to the elf. "I'm sorry. I didn't know she was coming here."

My face burned, and I took a step back from the elf's house and peered into the surrounding trees. I could only assume a few minutes at most had passed in this realm since Tam's departure, and he'd been working towards convincing the elf to help him find where the children had gone. Wherever the fairies were, at least I knew their weakness. I held onto Tam's weapon in one hand, reaching for a knife with the other.

"What are you doing?" Tam asked. "Perry, put that away."

"This?" I held up the knife, confusion flooding me at his accusatory tone. "I'm going to find those kids."

"Iron!" The elf jumped violently. "You have iron."

"Yes ... so? Most weapons have iron in them." Not Tam's, though, now that I thought about it. "I figured I might need to use it on whoever took those kids."

The elf backed away, shaking his head. "Not in here."

"What?" I blinked in surprise when the elf took off and

ran into the woods as fast as a vampire. I put the knife away, but he didn't reappear. "Wait a moment."

Tam stepped into my way. "Don't follow him. You'll make it worse."

Hot shame bubbled up inside me, but anger prevailed. "Worse than our team leader ditching us and leaving us to think he'd been kidnapped?"

"I told you to trust me, didn't I?"

"What was I supposed to think when I found this lying around?" I held up the stick in shaking hands. "We had no way to follow you, and Dylan said you were as good as dead."

"He doesn't have a clue what he's talking about."

"I'm glad there's one point you aren't arguing with me on." The world swayed beneath my feet, but it wasn't because of the fairies' magic. "What the hell has got into you?"

"I'm sorry, Perry," he said. "It's Dylan who is the problem. That was why I came here alone."

"What does that mean?" *Please, say something that makes sense. Please.*

"He was never looking for the fairies who took those children," he said. "Only the elf. And now we've given him exactly what he wants."

13

I stared at Tam. "What?"

"If Sylvan's left his realm, Dylan will be waiting for him outside." He strode across the clearing, while the pixie continued to fly in circles above our heads. "He intends to hand Sylvan over for a bounty from the hunters."

My jaw dropped. "What? Because he took the children?"

"No, of course not," he said. "The elf is innocent, but that doesn't matter to the hunters, does it? You should know that."

Yeah ... but that doesn't explain the rest. "Why did you want to come here alone, then?"

"Because Sylvan knows the other fairies, and I thought he'd be able to point me in their direction." He paced around the side of the cottage. "He said they were in a different part of their realm and he'd been avoiding them, but I didn't have the chance to ask him how to get there from here."

Before I showed up. My insides twisted with guilt, but at the same time, I wanted desperately to know *why* he'd deceived me and the rest of the team, and I didn't know how to voice the questions without turning each into an accusation.

"I wish you'd told us." I hated the pleading note in my voice. "Or at least told Kellen or someone at the office your plan, if not the rest of us."

"I hadn't figured out my plan before we left," he said. "I've been improvising, and besides—we haven't been able to get through to the office. Or did you manage to call them?"

"Yes, I did, and that was why I thought you ran into trouble." That and Dylan's comments, but the hunter might have been trying to wind me up, and I felt like a complete fool for falling for it. "Kellen told me that one of the signs pointing at the fairies was a circle of toadstools and that they were all over the forest."

Tam inhaled. "The fairy rings. Was that how you got in—no, you said you followed the pixie, didn't you?"

I followed his gaze to the little winged creature, which continued to fly around in agitation, no doubt still freaked out that it had been shut in the hunter's bag. "I did, but that was my next plan. Or it would have been, if the hunter hadn't been grabbing every toadstool he could find. How likely is that to backfire on him?"

"Fairly likely, if the fairies catch him." Tam shook his head. "He's more of a fool than I realised."

"That's right." Relief swept through me at our return to common ground. "He's cutting off all the other routes in and out of the fairies' world. That was why I didn't think you'd be able to get out."

"There are other ways," he said. "The fairies can see them."

That didn't mean *we* could, but Tam hadn't been alone here. He'd been with Sylvan, before I'd scared him off. "What about those kids, then? Are you sure they aren't in here?"

"No." He faced me, his mouth turning down at the corners. "Sylvan said they weren't. I don't have time to give you a crash course in how the fairies' realms work, and frankly, I don't understand a lot of it myself, but each realm or territory can be separated from the others. Sometimes there are ways to cross between them, sometimes not."

"Does that mean we might be able to get to the place where the children are being held captive from here?" I gestured to the trees behind the cottage. "Using another fairy ring?"

"No." His tone was deceptively soft, yet that simple word scraped at the inside of my chest like a scalpel. "You aren't coming with me, Perry. This isn't the world you're used to."

His tone rang with some emotion I couldn't name, but the hint of condescension put me on the defensive. "I know that, but dammit, Tam. I'm trying to help."

He knew that, but evidently, he didn't need me. If he had, he wouldn't have left me behind. And while he'd left the others, too, would he have looked at *them* with this level of horror if he'd seen them standing before him? I didn't know.

I was no stranger to rejection. My curse made that inevitable, but I'd foolishly begun to think that with Tam, it was different. He'd accepted me into the team despite my history, after all, and I must have internalised that acceptance more than I'd understood consciously.

Until he'd thrown it back in my face.

Without waiting for his reply, I turned my back and walked away from the elf's house. My eyes stung, and I furiously blinked at the threatening tears, willing myself to get a grip. *Even if he won't accept my help, those children are in danger. I have to help them.*

"Perry," Tam called after me. "Wait. Don't go off alone in here."

"*You're* alone in here," I snapped. "I'll leave you to it. Wasn't that what you wanted?"

The notion of spending another minute under his

judgmental stare was too much to bear. I didn't know if I'd be able to find my way out on foot, but the pixie was currently flying around in circles in a blur that put the vampire to shame. The odds of catching this pixie were nonexistent, which made me wonder how the hunter had managed it. He did have a few tricks up his sleeve, though. If he'd caught Sylvan too … okay, *that* part was my fault.

The rest, though? I hadn't cursed myself, and I was out of ideas about why else Tam could possibly be so horrified at my presence.

I crossed the clearing and picked a random path to enter the trees, but Tam soon caught up to me with his longer stride. "You won't find your way out through there."

I halted. "Don't give me any more of your condescension. I get it. I screwed up. Just show me the way out, and I'll leave you alone."

"I can't," he said. "Sylvan has left, and he's the only person who can navigate this area without running into anything else that might have made its home in here."

"You've got to be kidding me." I was stuck here with a guy who didn't even want to look at me. Just wonderful. "Fine. I'll get the iron out again."

I spied a promising-looking path and walked that way, certain that the village ought to be nearby. Granted, this place had no relation to the real world, and any door I found out of here might lead to the middle of the ocean for all I knew. That should be geographically impossible, but since when did the fairies care about logic?

I gave a startled yelp when my feet sank into watery ground, wondering if my thoughts had conjured up an *actual* ocean—but it was just another swamp. Hearing Tam's footsteps behind me, I waded onward until the water rose to my ankles.

"Perry—stop," Tam called after me. "If we're separated, we might not be able to find each other again."

I thought that was what you wanted. I tugged my feet out of the swamp, one at a time, as the sound of rushing water filled my ears. My head snapped up to see a river had appeared ahead of us.

"More glamour?" I guessed, stepping back, but my feet sank deeper with each step. The entire path was submerged, and the only way ahead lay on the other side of the river. It was huge, deeper than the brook we'd seen in the real world, and I wondered at the powerful magic that had hidden every inch of it.

"Don't go near that river," Tam warned. "We'll find another way around."

"I thought there was no 'we.'" A loud splash sounded, and my heart jumped into my throat when movement stirred in the water.

A sinuous dark shape swam towards us, lifting a horselike head out of the river. *Almost* like a horse—if horses could swim and had teeth like knives. "What in hell is that?"

"Perry ... we have to get out of here," Tam whispered. "Kelpies are very territorial."

Kelpies. I'd seen one or two before, but I could have sworn this monster was bigger and looked more vicious. "This is their home?"

"They aren't native to our world." He backed up a few steps, his feet sloshing in the swampy water, and I reluctantly followed.

The kelpie had already spotted us, however. With a whinny, it reared up, its hooves scarcely touching the ground as the waters parted around its body.

"We're not trespassing." I shuffled farther back. "We're not in the river, see? We'll go."

The beast roared, a sound that shook the treetops. I

reached for my wand, but before I could take aim, Tam had planted himself between the beast and me.

Seconds later, a wave rose from the river and crashed down upon Tam and me like a waterfall. I staggered, drenched, my vision blurred. Even with water clouding my eyes, I saw the beast lunging towards me—

Teeth snapped inches from my head as Tam *leapt.* He landed on the beast's back, gripping its long mane with both hands to keep from being thrown off.

"Tam!" I pulled out my wand, but I didn't dare fire a spell in case I hit him by mistake. The giant horse shook its head furiously, but Tam held fast, refusing to let go.

Damn. He was unarmed—I still had his weapon in my pocket—but if I tried to reach him, the kelpie would likely bite off my hand. I lifted my wand, my free hand inching towards my pocket, but just then, Tam lost his grip on the kelpie's back. The horse's head swung, sending him sprawling to the ground, and then its teeth sank into his jacket. Hissing and growling, the kelpie began dragging him across the marshy ground towards the river.

"Tam!" I let go of his weapon and grabbed my knife instead as the kelpie retreated to the water's edge, its teeth clamped over the back of Tam's jacket. He was lucky it hadn't bit his head instead, but I vaguely recalled that kelpies preferred to drown their victims.

Not happening. I marched towards the river, brandishing the iron knife. When the kelpie saw my weapon, it let out a chilling cry. Tam twisted free of its teeth and rolled onto his side, and I took aim.

"Leave us alone." The knife flew from my grip, and the kelpie plunged beneath the water. Another wave rose, drenching me to the skin. Spluttering, I blinked to clear my vision and saw Tam stagger away from the river, equally soaked.

"Did I hit it?" I coughed, swiping the back of my hand over my eyes.

"No. It swam off."

I swore. "That was one of my best knives."

"I wouldn't advise you to jump into the water to get it out."

"I guess not." I gave a short laugh, my teeth chattering with cold. "If this is all an illusion, it feels pretty bloody real to me."

"It's not an illusion. We're in the fairies' realm now, like I said. They play by different rules."

"Is this … where the children are?" If so, the odds were depressingly high that that monster had eaten them.

"No," he said. "Sylvan said they weren't near his house."

"Are you sure you trust the word of someone who keeps a kelpie in his back garden?"

"Well…" He paused. "You make a good point."

A strangled laugh escaped me, despite myself. Our brush with death had momentarily dwarfed our argument, but I couldn't forget the mess that had brought us here in the first place. Nor could I forget that he'd wanted me gone.

I reached into my pocket and pulled out the weapon I'd put away. "I should give you this back."

He took the sharpened stick from me with a murmured thanks. Water ran off his hand, trailing brightness, and I blinked to clear my vision again. Tam's form was slightly blurred, and although I might have appreciated the way the water plastered his clothes to his skin, I was more concerned that he appeared to be *glowing*.

"Tam," I said. "What…?"

"What is it?" He looked at me, his eyes a brighter green than usual, as I took in other subtle differences. His ears appeared more pointed than before, while his skin glittered and not simply with water droplets.

"Tam, you're glittering." A startled third laugh died in my throat as panic gripped me. "You look like—"

A fairy.

I began to back away from him, acutely aware that I was alone with someone who *almost* looked like Tam but wasn't him. He'd been replaced, and I hadn't even noticed.

"Perry." He matched my steps one for one, and with every movement, my anger and fear festered. He didn't even *walk* like a human anymore.

"How long were you pretending to be him?" I spat at him. "Who are you?"

"Perry, you don't understand," he said. "This is me."

"Impossible." More water slid off his clothes, and a pair of wings unfurled from his back. "What the hell?"

"Dammit." He swore and snapped his fingers, and a shimmering haze swept over him like a curtain. When the light cleared, his face was back to normal, his ears no longer pointed, his eyes no longer glowing. "Sorry. I didn't know being here would have that effect. The water must have washed away the—"

"Glamour." I didn't dare move any closer to him, even though he was wearing the face I knew well. "Nice try. You can't fool me, though. What did you do with the real Tam?"

"I told you, this is me." He lowered his hand. "This wasn't how I wanted you to find out. Hell, I didn't want you to know at all."

"You're twisted," I said shakily. "You were out to take advantage of us from the start, weren't you? When did you take his place? When we first arrived in the village?"

A thought pierced my shock, briefly—if the only way out of here was for a fairy to show me the exit, this guy seemed committed enough to the act that he might do me the favour. But how could I ever trust someone who wore the face of a friend? Even a friend I'd argued with recently—but had that even been him at all?

"Perry." He reached out a hand then lowered it, his expression conflicted. "What can I do to convince you it's me?"

"Get me the hell out of here, for a start," I said. "Then bugger off and bring back the real Tam."

"Illusion can't recreate memories," he said. "That's beyond the capabilities of glamour. I can remember when we met, Perry. You showed up at the tower not realising you'd been assigned to a team."

"Anyone could have told you that." My heart sank more with each word. "You really are despicable, do you know that?"

"On our last mission, the inspector got possessed by a demon."

"Again. That's in our records."

No fairy could have accessed them, though, and even the rest of us had had trouble getting hold of the office in the past couple of days... but if he'd been following us around, he would have had ample opportunity to listen to the team's conversations.

Wait. Surely a fairy couldn't have followed us back to the tower yesterday. He wouldn't have been able to fool everyone on the team, and he wouldn't have known the way to the village either. That meant he must have been waiting here for me specifically ... unless he'd taken Tam's place after the moment I'd stormed off.

But why would he have helped me fight off the kelpie? To gain my trust?

"You beat me at Scrabble last time," he said. "With the word 'goblin.'"

"You can't know that." Not if it wasn't Tam. Not if he wasn't—

"It's me, Perry," he repeated. "It's always been me."

Oh. Oh god. Tam was really…

He was a fairy.

"Then you…" My throat became dry. "You were wearing glamour the entire time we knew one another."

Impossible. I would have noticed, or one of the others would have figured it out…

Or would they? He carefully dodged certain questions, I'd never found out what type of paranormal he was, and Maurice couldn't read his thoughts.

How well did I know Tam, really?

"I don't have time to explain it all now," he said. "I never meant to deceive you, but we still have two children to save, and that Dylan… If he's caught Sylvan, it's not going to help the situation."

Right. The missing children. Tam had said they weren't here, but could I trust his word when he hadn't even worn his real face the entire time that we'd known one another?

Did I have a choice?

"Okay." I nodded, mechanically. "We'll find the hunter, and then … I want answers."

"Fair enough." A measure of resignation flitted across his face. "I'll explain when this is over."

Will this ever be over? Even if we solved this case, the team was under investigation already, and…

"They don't know." The words tripped over one another on the way out of my mouth. "The others don't know, do they?"

A long pause. "No … no, they don't, and now isn't the right time to tell them."

"Why not?" A sudden rush of anger arose in me, as did the burning need to know why he'd gone to such lengths to hide a major part of himself. "You're their team leader, aren't you? You've known them for longer than you've known me."

"That's true." He drew in a breath. "I'd like to be the one to tell them. If you'll let me."

"I didn't mean…" What did I mean? This was too confusing. The part of me that was hurt by the way he'd brushed me off and left me behind warred with the nagging voice in my head telling me that he never made decisions without good reason. Even keeping a secret this monumental from the rest of the team. "Never mind. Can you get us out of here?"

"If that's what you want." He stepped past me without making eye contact. Even in his human disguise, he moved far more gracefully than anyone I'd known who wasn't a vampire. My instincts had told me he wasn't like Maurice, but somehow the truth had shaken me even more than the idea of him being an immortal. Fairies *were* immortal, though, weren't they?

God, it was a good job I'd never foolishly acted on the crush I'd developed on him. He probably didn't even *like* humans in that way.

We walked in silence for a few moments, leaving the river far behind us. As the tension grew to an unbearable peak, Tam slowed his pace. "We're close."

I didn't see anything, but Tam's gaze roved up and down as if he was following a movement I couldn't detect. Then he snapped his fingers, which made me jump, and beckoned.

As I followed him, the swampy water vanished, and so did the weird glittering sheen over the trees that I hadn't even noticed before. Everything was suddenly duller in colour, and the murmur of voices reached my ears.

"There." Relief filled his voice. "I knew it couldn't be far off."

"Right." I didn't see any markers or toadstools, but there didn't need to be any. Not when his eyes could see through glamour while mine couldn't.

If I wanted to ask him anything more, now was the time,

but he'd already said he'd explain later, and in the end, I couldn't trust myself not to open my mouth and make everything worse. The aftermath of our last argument was too raw.

And I had no idea how to fix things.

14

T am and I walked a short distance down the path before we found the rest of the team outside the clearing where the elf's house had been.

When she saw me, Farley jumped to her feet. "Perry ... *Tam!*"

"You're okay." Callum ran over to us. "Wait, why are you both soaking wet?"

"Fell in a river." My voice barely shook, for a wonder. "A river with a man-eating horse living in it."

"A man-eating horse?" Maurice asked. "Was that what chased Sylvan off?"

"Sylvan... He ran away." My relief at seeing the rest of the team dimmed at the reminder of my failures. "He ran away, and without him, the fairy realm ... changed. Did you see him?"

"He ran that way." Callum pointed. "Dylan was chasing him."

Dammit. Tam was right. "None of you went after him?" I kept an eye on Maurice when I asked that question, since the vampire was probably the only one who could have been able to keep pace with the speedy elf.

Maurice, however, just shrugged. "Serves the elf right if the hunter caught him."

"Sylvan wasn't the one who took those kids," I told him. "He was trying to help Tam find them…"

The weight of Tam's stare on my back pushed me into silence. If I stuck to my word and didn't tell the others his secret, I wouldn't be able to explain *why* he thought the elf was innocent, save for his word. That might be enough for the rest of the team, but the others didn't know the extent of the secrets Tam kept.

"Then we have to find him," Callum decided. "I did wonder why Dylan took off like that, but the guy was a weirdo who captured a pixie in a bag. Where'd it go, anyway?"

"We left the pixie behind, I think." I still wasn't best pleased with the little creature for tricking small children into walking into a trap, but my encounter with the kelpie had highlighted how much more dangerous the fairies' realm could be.

"You followed it into the fairies' home, didn't you?" Farley said. "That was how you got there."

"Yeah… I asked it to take me to the children, which it didn't, but I don't think it could understand a word I said."

"We heard." Maurice eyed me with a mixture of disdain and what I could only describe as bewildered awe. "You're even more of a reckless weirdo than I thought. Who walks into a fairy realm on purpose?"

"There's no other way to get the children back, as well you know." I shook water off my sleeves, taking care to splash it in the vampire's direction, and he scowled in response.

"Exactly," Callum said. "Can we get there without the

pixie, do you know? If Dylan left any toadstools behind to follow, I suppose we can find one of those fairy rings..."

"We don't need those." When the others all looked at me, my heart dropped. I'd spoken without thinking, but it was impossible to explain that Tam could see through glamour without giving away his secret. "I mean, Sylvan can lead us there if we find him. Right, Tam?"

"*If* we find him." Tam's tone had no hint of emotion, no hints that he'd detected that I'd almost slipped up. "If he's outrun the hunter, we'll have to catch him first."

"That won't be an issue," said Maurice, exposing his fangs. "I can catch them both. And I know iron works on fairies too."

Tam stiffened. "Don't harm Sylvan. Like I said, he wasn't the one who took those children."

"If you're sure." Farley glanced at me, a question in her eyes, and my heart sank even further. She must have picked up on some of the weird vibes between Tam and me, but I hoped she wouldn't ask for details yet. I needed to get my head on straight—and finding the elf and the hunter was our priority. I didn't know whether Dylan had actually caught the elf yet, but either way, the vampire ought to be able to find them both without too much exertion.

Maurice glided ahead of us through the trees, and we followed his lead. I avoided both Callum and Farley's attempts to catch my eye, but the only way to stay out of speaking distance was to walk next to Tam, and I couldn't meet his gaze either. Emotions warred within me, as much as I tried to tamp them down—mostly so Farley wouldn't get any more suspicious than she already was. I hadn't a clue if Tam was half as conflicted, though for all I knew, Farley couldn't sense his feelings at all. Like Maurice couldn't read his thoughts.

And now I suspected I knew why ... fairies must be

immune to mind reading. More clues I'd overlooked. Or ignored. Because I hadn't wanted to rock the boat, hadn't wanted to upend the fragile unity of our newly formed team. I'd assumed, foolishly, that my own secret was the worst one on my team, to the extent that I'd looked straight past all the signs that Tam wasn't what he seemed.

How far did it go? How many little white lies had he told to protect his secret?

Hadn't I told as many myself, to keep the truth about my curse from getting out there?

Just when the silence was getting unbearable, Maurice came to a sudden halt—so abrupt that Callum almost bumped into him from behind. "Whoa. What is it?"

"That." Maurice pointed downward, and Tam hissed out a breath. Several toadstools sprouted around the path on either side of us, forming a circle... which we'd unknowingly walked straight into.

Where did they come from?

"Did they just grow out of nowhere?" Callum swivelled on his heel, bafflement underlying his voice.

"No ... they must have been hidden by glamour." I looked at Tam, wondering why he hadn't seen them—and horror flitted across his face.

"I wasn't paying attention." He swore. "I'm sorry. I should have known they'd try something like this."

"Who's 'they'?" asked Callum. "The fairies? I thought they only took children."

A high, chilling laugh rang out in the background.

"Who was that?" I looked for the source, but the trees closing in around the path masked everything else from view. "Damn. We're in the fairies' home."

"What?" Farley recoiled, shrinking behind Callum. "How'd we walk in here without knowing?"

At a second laugh, the hairs on my arms stood on end.

Although the laughter sounded more joyful than sinister, the very knowledge that I was in a realm full of creatures that were nothing but hostile to humans made my survival instincts kick in and urge me to run. Or fight.

"Never mind that," Maurice said. "How do we get out?"

"Well…" I looked at Tam, unable to help myself. After all, he was the only person in our group who could see through glamour to find the way back home … but if the children were in here, we needed to find them first.

Tam's mouth pressed into a thin line. "Remember why we came here. We need to find the missing children."

As another wave of laughter rang out, my blood iced over. That was a child's laughter.

"Joy?" I lifted my head and stepped forward, trying to track the sound's direction, and stiffened when Tam caught my arm.

"Watch out," he said. "It might be a trap."

My arm burned where he'd touched me, and he released me a moment later as if he'd felt my reaction. As if this couldn't get any worse. I took in a sharp breath. "Right. The fairies are faking children's laughter, are they?"

"What?" Farley looked between us in bewilderment. "Are the children here or not?"

Callum made a noise of disgust. "Are the fairies seriously imitating human children? That's creepy."

"This whole place is creepy," Maurice remarked. "Is it even real?"

"It's real but not in the sense that we're familiar with." Tam turned towards the path ahead, not looking back at me, and I did my best to squash down the emotions churning inside me. "Our best bet is to stay on the path and not to split up," Tam said.

The rest of us fell in behind him, all too happy to let him lead the way as we would in any other mission—but only I knew why he was so adamant that he needed to take the lead. He alone would be able to spot any oncoming obstacles the fairies had hidden, but the trees on either side remained uniform even as the chilling laughter continued. It *sounded* real, but that was the point, wasn't it? Fairies' illusions were so thorough that they could be mistaken for the real things.

Like Tam's. I found myself watching his back as we walked. His posture was tense, without a wing or pointed ear to be seen. How had he learned to cast such a convincing illusion? Fairies must be born with the ability, but did they have the fairy equivalent of magical academies that taught the skills to survive in the human world? Questions buzzed in my mind, none of which I could voice aloud.

Tam slowed his pace and held out a hand. "Stay back. Hide in those bushes."

"From what?" Confusion filled Callum's voice. "I don't see any bushes."

Neither did I, but the laughter drifted in as if someone had turned up the volume on an imaginary device. An instant later, bushes sprang up ahead of us as if they'd simply popped out of the ground.

On the other side of the bushes lay a clearing—and in the centre, two children danced in circles. I stopped in my tracks, heart in my throat. *Joy. Lloyd.* They were … dancing?

"What the hell?" Callum whispered. "How long have they been here?"

"Shh," Tam hissed. "They aren't alone."

What—? I squinted at the children, who were haloed in bright light—and then my eyes picked out several other figures nearby. Two pointy-eared, winged figures, the same size as the children, danced with them, and glitter showered the ground. My eyes followed the movement as the children swirled and danced and laughed, but the longer I looked, the more clearly I saw the exhaustion on the human children's faces. Yet their feet kept moving, kept dancing. *How long have they been there?*

"It's an enchantment," Tam muttered. "I don't know if it'll wear off by itself when we get them out of here."

"How're we supposed to do that?" Especially without drawing attention? I glimpsed two other figures at the edge of the clearing, taller than the ones dancing in the centre. The pair watched the dancing children with apparent fascination or amusement, not seeming to notice our presence at all.

"Stay hidden," Tam said. "I'll talk to them."

Even Maurice obeyed, ducking out of sight amid the bushes with the rest of us. A voice in the back of my mind screamed at me not to leave Tam to handle the fairies alone, despite my better instincts reminding me that he was far more qualified than the rest of us. He alone understood them.

Tam left the bushes behind and strode towards the clearing. The dancing fairies didn't appear to notice him at first. That or they didn't care.

"Excuse me," Tam called out. "Those children belong to the humans."

One of the small pointy-eared figures turned to him. "Have you come to dance?"

"No," Tam said, his voice clear. "Those are human children. They aren't yours. Let them go."

"Where's your sense of fun?" A smaller fairy skipped over to his side and tried to grab his hand, and Tam smoothly stepped out of reach. "Come and dance."

"No." Tam repeated the word, keeping his attention on the children. While he wasn't in his own fairy form, the glitter showering the area clung to his skin and made it easy to imagine him with his wings out, dancing alongside them.

Next to me, the other team members didn't make any comment, so I didn't know if they'd noticed as well.

My heart lurched when one of the two taller figures made their way over to Tam, wings beating.

"Now, that isn't very nice of you," said the fairy, in melodic tones. Seeing him up close, I'd put him as male and his companion as female. "Why do you want to ruin my children's fun?"

"They're your children?" Tam paused to consider the three smaller fairies, who circled their human captives in an endless dance. "You must understand why the humans want theirs back. They care for their young as well."

"The humans stepped onto our land," said the male fairy. "They owe us in exchange. Besides, the small humans *want* to dance."

"Only because you bewitched them," Tam said. "What do you mean, 'stepped onto our land'?"

"The forest was ours first." The second fairy—female, long-haired—flew over and joined the male. "The humans moved in and built their houses, and we let them, but we couldn't ignore the latest insult."

"Insult?" Tam was silent for an instant. "The elf, you mean?"

"The elves are wicked and deceptive," hissed the male fairy. "They don't belong in our forest."

"The elves might say the same of you," Tam said evenly.

What? The elves and fairies don't get along? I didn't know why that surprised me, since the other paranormals tended to have rivalries too. Just look at vampires and werewolves. And shifters and other shifters. Not to mention the Wardens and the paranormal hunters. Did Sylvan have any idea that his presence in town had kicked up this much controversy?

"When we went to see the elf, our children told us they

were bored," said the male fairy. "They wanted friends to play with, and so we found some. See how willing they are?"

"You bewitched them," Tam said. "You must know you can't hold them here forever. The humans want them back."

"The humans can come and bargain with us, then," said the female fairy. "Do you presume to speak for them?"

Be careful, Tam. I had to wonder if the other fairies recognised him as one of them or were just humouring him. Either way, I didn't trust them to hold to any bargain they made.

"I have an idea," said the male fairy. "We can offer an exchange. Two of ours for two of yours."

Tam stiffened. "What does that mean?"

"Two of ours." The male fairy gestured to the dancing children. "For two of yours."

Then he pointed straight at the bushes where we were hidden.

15

All the attention turned towards our hiding place. The second adult fairy took flight in a beat of her gossamer wings and hovered above the bushes in which we crouched. A smile graced her pointed face. "Humans, hiding in the bushes? Let's see what we have here."

I reached for my weapon, but thorns stabbed my arms as the bushes came to life around us. I yelped, springing forward, and heard Farley scream next to me. Callum swore, hitting out at the bushes, only to become further entangled. I wrapped my arms around myself to shield my body and ran forward blindly—until a pair of hands grabbed my shoulders and lifted me into the air.

"Let go of me." I squirmed, kicking out, but the fairy had a surprisingly strong grip.

"You don't want the thorns to catch you, human, do you?" Her soft melodic voice contrasted with the sharp nails digging into my arms.

I glanced down at the bushes, from which the second fairy emerged with a struggling Farley in his grip. Nearby, Callum fought his way through the thorns, but Maurice had vanished. *Damn him.* The vampire had evidently taken the easy way out—but was there any escaping this place?

"Don't fight it, human," said the fairy, planting my feet on the ground. "Forget all your troubles and dance."

The children—both human and fairy—had started to dance again, moving in a whirl of limbs and glitter. As the adult fairy holding me attempted to push me towards them, I dug my heels into the ground with all the strength I could muster. Next to me, the male fairy placed a limp-looking Farley into the clearing. The instant her feet touched the ground, she began to dance as well, limbs jerking, head lolling.

"Let her go!" I snarled, hearing Callum shouting in the background too. Where was Maurice? If he was planning to stage a rescue mission, I might forgive him for running off, but the alarming part was that Tam had also disappeared.

"There's no point in trying to escape us, mortal," murmured the female fairy. "Just relax and listen to the music…"

"What music?"

The words hadn't left my mouth before I heard it—a tinkling tune like delicate fingers on an unseen piano. The music wrapped around me, echoing in my ears and humming in my veins. My limbs began to move, unbidden, and all thoughts left my mind. Everything except the desire to keep dancing.

The desire consumed me, took hold of every cell in my body. Why had I resisted again? Even Farley was enjoying herself, throwing her head back and laughing as we danced, as were Joy and Lloyd. Hands grabbed me from behind, and I pushed them away, continuing to dance.

When the hands tried to grab me again, I trod on the owner's feet.

"Dammit," a muffled voice said. "Maurice—can you grab her?"

"I thought you wanted to get the kids out of here first," came the sullen response.

"Yes—fine, I'll get them myself."

I knew that voice. I tried to tilt my head to see its owner, but my feet continued to lurch out of my control, and the dance seemed less fun than before. The music faded in and out as I tried to focus on the two strange voices. Then a blurred figure stepped in front of me, knocking me off balance. As I stumbled, hands seized me from behind and *yanked* me off my feet.

The world tilted sideways, and a startled gasp escaped from me as the clearing lurched past and trees and glitter whirled around me in an inexplicable blur.

When the hands released me, I fell flat on my face—or I would have, if the person who'd dragged me away from the clearing hadn't grabbed my arm again at the last moment. His sharp grip should have shocked me back to my senses, but the faint traces of music in the background threatened to seize my limbs and coax me into dancing again.

"Pull yourself together," he snapped. "I need one of you to come to your senses so I can help Tam."

Tam. The name jolted me to my core with the effect of a bucket of ice-cold water upended over my head. I breathed hard, no longer hearing the music, but I was so dizzy that my knees buckled, and my eyes refused to focus on my surroundings. I didn't need to be able to see my rescuer to know who it was, though it seemed impossible that *Maurice* of all people had come to save me. "Vampires are immune…"

"To fairies' magic, I know," Maurice growled. "Shifters too. Are you going to stop doing that stupid dance now?"

Lifting my head, I saw Callum dragging a struggling Farley out of the clearing, and behind them—*Tam*. His tall figure was visible above the bushes, but I couldn't see whether he'd succeeded in getting hold of either of the two human children.

"I'm okay," I slurred. "Help him."

Why did it have to be Maurice? Farley was in a state, too, flailing around in Callum's arms; no doubt the fairies' music was amplified for her, especially since she could feel all our emotions too. Maurice glided past them, and I heard the fairy children shriek in protest. I could only assume that he and the others had taken the adult fairies out of commission, but my wobbling feet and dizziness made it hard to pinpoint my own location, let alone anyone else's.

Maurice reappeared with a struggling child in his arms. *Joy.* Behind him, Tam held Lloyd, who continued to kick out feebly.

"Let's go." The vampire strode into the lead, easily keeping his grip on Joy. I tried to keep up but kept tripping, my legs jerking out of my control. Since Callum was occupied with holding Farley and the kids needed help more than I did, I continued grimly onward until the dizziness passed enough for me not to fall over my own feet.

"Tam." I gasped out his name. "Ah—what did you do to the adult fairies?"

A flutter of wings behind answered for me. *Oh boy.*

"Knocked them out," Callum answered, holding a limp Farley in his arms. "I think they woke up."

More wingbeats pursued us—a reminder that the fairies also possessed a significant advantage over the rest of us and that there was no escaping them in their own home. I kept moving, anger spurring me onward. I wouldn't let them put me under their spell again, and I sure as hell wouldn't let them take the children.

Gritting my teeth, I reached into my pocket for my

weapon, and as the wings descended, I spun around. This time, I brandished the iron knife with no fear.

"Get away from us!" I shouted. "I have iron."

The two fairies stopped midflight with screeches of outrage. Encouraged, I waved the knife to left and right, as if I was deciding who to throw it at. Out of the corner of my eye, I saw my teammates disappear around a corner, but Tam remained behind.

"This way!" he called to me. "Perry—get out of here. I'll follow."

Reluctantly, I obeyed. Keeping a tight grip on the iron knife, I backed towards him, one eye fixed on the fairies. Once I was certain they weren't about to dive-bomb me, I followed Tam and ducked around a corner.

There, I came to a startled halt. I was back in the forest— the *real* forest—as evidenced by the houses visible through gaps in the trees. Nearby, Farley had finally stopped fighting Callum's hold long enough for him to put her down, and the two children sat huddled together next to an unimpressed-looking Maurice. The fairies' cries had faded into the background, as if the pair had never existed.

"How—?" A mixture of relief and dread flooded me when Tam stepped into view. "Please tell me the fairies didn't follow you out."

"No." He indicated the village. "They're still wary of the humans, and there are too many of us for them to fight against, especially when we have iron."

"Damn right." I staggered over to Callum and Farley and crouched next to them to catch my breath. My legs ached from the forced dance, but the humiliation burning in my lungs was worse. The fairies had played me like a fiddle, and I'd barely been able to put up a fight.

"We're back home." Callum sighed, leaning back against a

tree. "We have the kids. Please tell me it's over. I never want to see that place again."

Same. I was surprised none of the others had asked the obvious question yet, but maybe I shouldn't have been. Of course *I* knew how Tam had found the way out—not to mention why he'd been immune to the spell—but they were likely too relieved to question our miraculous escape.

"It's not quite over," said Tam, eyeing the two exhausted children. "But for them, it is. Can you take them back to their parents? I need to sort something out here."

"What?" Farley croaked. "You're not going back *there*, are you?"

"No… I'm going after Dylan," he explained. "He won't be able to take credit for finding the children, but he's set on getting Sylvan blamed for this, and the last thing we need is more hunters swarming into town."

"Wasn't it Sylvan who technically caused the fairies to get all territorial in the first place?" I pointed out.

Tam didn't meet my eyes. "Not intentionally, and he'll be unable to resolve the matter if the hunters lock him up. Or worse."

True, but conflicting thoughts battled in my mind as Callum and Farley helped the two frightened children to their feet.

"Come on, we'll take you home," Callum told them. "It's not far now."

While they began to coax Joy and Lloyd out of the forest, Maurice lingered behind. "Still want me to find that hunter? I don't care about the elf, but I'd be happy to make him sorry he crossed us."

"No," said Tam. "I'd rather do this alone."

Not this again. I figured I knew why Tam wanted to talk to the elf by himself, but I didn't trust Dylan one bit. And despite the shock of Tam's revelation, part of me refused to let our team leader walk into another trap.

"The last time you tried to act alone, you got lost in the fairies' realm," said Maurice, who'd presumably been thinking along the same wavelength. "I can be your backup. If Dylan tries to run, I'll catch him."

Tam exhaled in a sigh. "All right, but let me talk to him first."

"And me," I added. "I have some questions for him too."

Tam gave me a look of surprise but didn't comment in front of the vampire. In truth, I didn't know why I was helping Tam when he'd acted as if I'd mortally insulted him by coming to help the last time—not to mention the way he'd deceived all of us about his real identity. Maybe I wanted to make up for the former, but I couldn't make sense of the latter. Not without asking for an explanation … which he'd promised me, after this was over.

I intended to ensure he kept his word.

Without arguing, Tam let the vampire scout ahead while the two of us walked in silence. The atmosphere was not quite as tense as the last time but a far cry from our former camaraderie. Luckily, Maurice soon returned to our side. "He's ahead. And he … he has the elf tied up."

Tam swore under his breath. "Of course he does."

We followed Maurice's lead for a short distance until Tam overtook us both to talk to the hunter alone. Maurice and I remained concealed behind the nearby trees, which reminded me uncomfortably of hiding in the bushes in the fairies' realm. I stood back rather than going deeper among the leaves, just in case the thorns came to life and attacked me again, though at least this time our adversary was human.

I peered through the branches and saw the elf lying at the base of a tree in an uncomfortable-looking position that suggested the hunter had tied Sylvan's arms behind his back.

Dylan himself paced around the clearing, a mobile phone pressed to his ear.

"Can't get a bloody signal in here," he muttered to himself. "Hey—you."

He'd spotted Tam, who approached the hunter without a hint of fear in his expression. "Dylan. You've captured an innocent man."

"What's it to you?" the hunter retaliated.

"It's over," Tam said. "We found the missing children with their real captors. Sylvan wasn't in any way involved."

"Does it matter?" Dylan cocked a brow. "The police can't see the fairies. They won't know any better, will they?"

"You're despicable," said Tam in a low voice, and I felt a surge of emotion I hadn't expected. The desire to step up and face down the hunter beside him warred with the knowledge that he wouldn't want me to give away my presence here.

"Do you think I care what you think?" Dylan stepped forwards. "I'd advise you to walk away before you get yourself into trouble."

The threat chilled me, but I realised that Maurice was no longer at my side. I glanced over to the other side of the clearing, where the vampire stealthily approached the elf from behind.

I kept one eye on him and one on Tam, who said, "Think carefully before you threaten a Warden, Dylan. You don't want to get yourself into trouble either."

"Would anyone know?" He smirked. "There's no phone signal out here. You can't contact your supervisors, and it's not like there aren't other dangers in the forest, is it? Would they believe I was responsible for anything that might happen to you … or would they be more likely to blame the fairies instead?"

The elf gave a startled movement when he caught sight of the vampire. "Oh!"

The hunter made to turn his way, and on impulse, I stepped out to join Tam. "Oh, they'd believe you're a piece of crap, Dylan. Don't forget Tam isn't here alone."

Dylan didn't look fazed in the slightest, but at least he'd looked away from the elf. The hunter reached into his pocket and pulled out a device that looked like a gun but was smaller and shinier. "Know what this is?"

"One of those silver bullet guns?" I watched Maurice undoing the elf's bonds out of the corner of my eye and raised my voice to keep the hunter's eyes on my face. "For shooting werewolves?"

"Better." He grinned. "The bullets in this are made of iron. Cold iron."

My blood iced over. Did he … did he know what Tam was? Not that it mattered, since a bullet would bring down a human as easily as it would a fairy, but I could only imagine how he might hold that knowledge over our heads.

"Bullets don't make you immune to magic." Tam's voice, like his expression, held no hint of fear. "They don't make up for your own deficiencies."

Ha. The hunter made to speak, and bushes rustled in the background. He spun to face his captive—who was no longer there—as I glimpsed the vampire disappearing into the trees with the startled elf in his arms.

"How dare you!" the hunter shouted. "You'll pay for that."

Quick as a flash, I drew my wand and pointed it at the gun in Dylan's hand. My spell blasted the weapon from his grip, and Tam glided behind him, his sticklike instrument raised high. One swing, and Dylan crumpled to the ground into a heap.

Tam straightened upright. "That was easier than I expected."

I grinned despite myself and strode to his side. "Not very bright, is he?"

Tam crouched down and picked up the gun-like instrument carefully. "This needs to be taken care of. I'll contact his supervisors."

"We can always drop him on their doorstep on the way back." I spied Dylan's bag lying nearby and picked it up too. "I bet there's all kinds of crap in here as well. Better make sure he hasn't picked up anything else that's alive."

"Let's see." Tam leaned over the bag, and tension bloomed between us once more. We were alone, or as alone as was possible with an unconscious hunter nearby, and yet ... and yet I still didn't know what to say.

I opened the bag instead and tipped out the contents. Weapons, yes ... and toadstools. "Will the fairies come after him for this, do you think?"

"They might," Tam said. "We've made enemies of them ourselves now."

Oh. Yeah, I kinda threatened them with iron.

"Not all of them." Maurice reappeared with the dazed elf in tow. "What do you want me to do with him?"

"Let him go." Tam peered at Sylvan's confused face. "Are you all right?"

"Never better." The elf spotted the fallen hunter. "What happened to him? Hit his head, did he?"

"With help." Belatedly, I remembered my last encounter with Sylvan and was glad I'd put my weapons away. "Erm, I'm sorry about earlier."

The elf, to my consternation, burst out laughing. "The foolish human."

Still chuckling, he ambled away, while the vampire looked between Tam and me as if trying to figure out what I'd apologised for. Ack. I needed to steer the line of questioning away from *that* as fast as possible.

Tam got there first. "Thanks for the help setting him free, Maurice."

The vampire shrugged. "I don't get why you think he's trustworthy, but whatever."

I heard the implicit meaning. He trusted Tam. So did the others, even though he was deceiving them … but would they see it that way? For that matter, did *I* see it that way? If I hadn't seen his mask slip, he would still be the same Tam I'd known all this time. Except for when he'd tried to push me away, he'd never given me reason to believe he was anyone else.

The thought of our argument brought a familiar rush of shame, but I hadn't exactly acted like the picture of decorum when the truth about my curse had come out either. All I knew was that the ache in my chest whenever I looked at him was too much to bear.

With a final scathing look at the hunter, the vampire departed for the village. Tam stayed still, though, and I heard the elf humming to himself in the background as he made his meandering way home.

"Are you sure you want to let him go and hide again?" I whispered to Tam. "I know he probably had no clue that the fairies started taking human children because they were annoyed that he moved here, but if that kelpie is still hanging around, it's a hazard to anyone who walks into his part of the woods."

"I'll talk to him," he said. "I just have something else I need to do first."

"What—?" I broke off. "Does it involve speaking to the fairies? Because it won't do any good if we leave town and they take another child as soon as we're gone."

"Exactly." He called to the elf. "Sylvan?"

"Yes?" The elf slowed his pace and let Tam catch up to him.

"Sylvan, I know you've had a shock, but the fairies wanted to talk to you as well," he said. "Is that all right with you?"

I raised a brow at him. "Did they? I thought they wanted him gone."

Tam gave me a warning look, while Sylvan's expression showed little more than confusion. "You did find those children, didn't you?" Sylvan asked.

"We did, yes," said Tam. "However, we need to ensure that the fairies never take any children captive again. Would you like to help?"

The elf considered him. "Very well."

As they both made to leave, Tam caught my eye. A question passed unspoken between us—*Do you want to stay? Or come with us?*

I didn't *want* to speak to the fairies again, but my need for answers won out. Besides, if the enemy made any more threats towards the villagers *or* my team, I had my iron knife handy.

16

I followed Tam and the elf a short distance through the trees, tensing when a fluttering noise sounded and the female fairy from earlier descended in a shower of glitter. When she saw me, she shrieked. "You!"

Glaring up at her, I reached for my knife again. "Leave those children alone. This is your last warning."

"Who cares about the children?" she spat. "You insulted and tricked us and rejected our bargain!"

"I'm not giving you any of my team members," Tam asserted. "Besides, I thought he was the one you wanted to talk to."

The fairy looked down at the elf, seeming to notice him for the first time. "You! The trespasser!"

"Trespasser?" The elf merely looked confused. "I don't remember you living in this village."

"Technically, he has a point there," I told the fairy. "You don't live in Pleasance Grove. Technically, you don't even live in the forest. Not the human one."

"The forest is ours!" the fairy said indignantly. "We were here first."

"Isn't there room enough for both of you?" Tam asked.

"Yeah, don't you and your children live alone in a bubble universe that can be as big as you want it to?" I added. "You can literally live in a world apart from everyone else if you want to without ever interacting with anyone but your own family."

Not the worst idea. If only it was that easy for me to avoid Maurice in the tower without one of us having to leave.

"Why is this human talking to us?" asked the female fairy. "This is none of the humans' business."

I thought she was addressing a nearby tree before I spotted the pixie who'd been lurking out of sight.

"You dragged the humans into this when you captured their children." I directed my words at both the pixie and the fairy. "You'll have a lot more to worry about than a single elf minding his own business in your forest if you get into the habit of stealing their kids."

"Is that a threat, mortal?" the fairy queried.

"No, it's the truth," said Tam. "You know that if the humans believe their children are endangered in the forest, they'll bring more humans—and iron too. They'll drive you out even if they don't mean to."

The fairy's wings beat, agitated. "Those humans and their unseeing eyes already built their houses on our land. Why should they be allowed to take what isn't theirs?"

My mouth opened. Had the village been on top of a fairy ring? Given the number of toadstools in the forest, it wasn't out of the realm of possibility, but I was sure the humans hadn't been aware of it.

"They didn't know," I said to her. "How could they have known you were here when you never showed your faces?"

"You haven't spent much time around humans, have you?"

Tam looked between her and Sylvan. "You two have more in common than you're aware of."

"No!" the fairy shrieked in a voice so high pitched that I covered my ears. "We left the courts because we did not care for the rules. Why should we submit to humans and live side by side with elves?"

"One elf, and he's harmless." He was too. Sylvan didn't appear to even realise he was being threatened. "He's retired here to get some peace. Isn't that true?"

"It's true, Sylvan, isn't it?" Tam added.

The elf nodded enthusiastically. "Retired? Yes, yes. I won't intrude."

The fairy huffed. "The humans will ask questions about you. It's only a matter of time before they find us too."

"You drew their attention to yourself by taking their children," I pointed out.

"We offered them a favour!" said the fairy indignantly. "The children got to experience dreams the likes of which few humans will ever set eyes on."

"Humans don't see things in the same way as you," said Tam. "If you take the time to educate yourself on them, they'll return the favour."

The fairy looked at him haughtily. "You're half in their world, divided one. How can you understand what it's like for us?"

"I understand what it's like to live outside the courts," Tam replied. "As for you and the elf, it must be possible to reach a compromise. Consider it."

The fairy huffed. "I will discuss this with my kin. And I will not forget your slight, human," she added to me, before vanishing in a swirl of glitter.

I blinked. "Does that mean we're mortal enemies, or ... or immortal ones?"

More to the point, what had the rest of their conversation been about? *Divided one? Outside the courts?* Maybe it was possible for humans to reach a point of understanding, but I was starting to wonder, again, if I'd ever known Tam at all.

My mouth went dry when I caught him watching me, his green eyes intent. Brighter than any human's I'd seen. His ears had a slight point at the edges that I hadn't detected either. I hadn't met many fairies before, but that was really no excuse for not noticing the obvious signs.

"What are you two doing?" Callum walked into view, banishing all questions from my mind. "Was that one of *them?*"

Farley hurried up alongside him, and her gaze locked on the elf. "Are you all okay?"

"Yeah." I saw Tam tense and wondered if he expected me to give away his secret, but I said, "They came back to negotiate. Well, kind of. The fairies don't really understand how humans work, and they're a little possessive over their forest."

"We noticed," Callum said dryly. "They aren't going to steal any more children, though?"

"I don't think they are." Tam eyed Sylvan. "I can trust you to keep an eye on them, can't I?"

"Oh, of course," the elf said cheerily. "I can talk to the humans right now, in fact."

"Erm." I looked at him, too, at his pointed ears and four-feet-tall frame. "With or without your glamour?"

———

The answer was 'without,' apparently. Glenn stared open-mouthed when Sylvan followed us into his office, and he kept staring at the elf while Tam gave him a summary of the events in the forest. Although nobody aside from our team and the elf was inside the police station, I could hear the villagers talking outside the front door.

Glenn took the news of the fairies' presence in the forest with less panic and more disbelief than I'd expected. "I don't know anything about any fairies. And I've lived here all my life."

"It's true," Tam said. "The fairies are invisible to human eyes, usually, so you wouldn't have known they were here."

"What am I supposed to do now?" he asked. "Tell everyone in the entire village that they have to avoid touching any mushrooms in the future?"

"Not every single toadstool in the forest," I said. "Just avoid ones that are placed in a circle."

That was my understanding anyway, which admittedly wasn't very extensive. The fairies might have any number of ways of ensnaring humans in their traps.

"And if you accidentally move a toadstool, just putting it back and apologising should be enough," said Tam. "I doubt the fairies would care if it was unintentional."

"They stole two children." Glenn glanced in the direction of the front door. "Some people won't forget that."

I gathered that Mr and Mrs Hutchins and Lloyd's parents were at home, too busy comforting their exhausted children to stay and talk. Good job, because I had an inkling that they wouldn't accept the fairies' excuse for their actions. Nor would they be impressed with Sylvan's cheery obliviousness. Mrs Hutchins might understand, but her husband was a different matter.

"He can help you explain everything to them." Tam indicated Sylvan, who was examining Glenn's laptop with an expression of rapt fascination. "If someone's willing to give him some lessons on how humans operate. He might need a few pointers."

"Iron!" the elf yelped, letting go of the laptop.

"And keep anything made of metal out of his way," I added, as my phone buzzed in my pocket. I checked and saw a message from Kellen. He'd sent it an hour ago, and it had only just come through.

I replied, saying I'd call him when I got back to the tower, needing to get my head on straight first. I wouldn't have minded an excuse to get out of this crowded room, but I didn't want to get swamped by locals either. I was bone tired, and thanks to running back and forth between the fairies' realm and this one, we'd lost most of a day again. The sky had darkened outside over the past hour, which didn't help my general exhaustion and my desire to go home.

Tam caught sight of my phone. "We need to report to our supervisor. They'll send someone to pick up that hunter too."

Glenn winced. "I didn't know he'd try to capture an innocent person."

"It didn't clue you in when he didn't even try looking for the children for two days?" I shook my head, neither expecting nor particularly wanting an answer. "Never mind. We'll report him, and if you need the Wardens again, I'd recommend getting in touch with our team."

"So do I." Tam gave me an approving look that made my heartbeat skitter. I'd correctly guessed that he'd prefer to be contacted personally if the villagers needed help negotiating with the inhabitants in the forest. Better than the Wardens' supervisors coming instead. Or worse ... the hunters. "Call me at the number I gave you."

Assuming he can get a signal. No doubt the fairies' presence in the forest played a part in their difficulties in contacting the outside world, but the signal seemed to have returned for the time being. When my phone buzzed again, I rose to my feet. Maurice had already left with an offer to keep an eye on the unconscious hunter, and I was all too happy to let Tam finish things up with Glenn and leave the office.

While several villagers lingered outside, they hardly paid me any attention, especially when they saw Sylvan.

"Is that an elf?" someone said.

"Where?" Sylvan swivelled around, and laughter drifted from nearby. The teenage girl from earlier found his reaction highly amusing, apparently. At least one person had seen his real form, but the rest of the villagers would have a bit of an adjustment to make.

Although I might have worried about their reactions, he was so obliviously cheerful that I didn't see how anyone could blame him for the kidnappings. Except for a certain hunter, of course.

"I'm glad that's over," Callum muttered as he walked out of the police station and joined me. "Does Tam really think the fairies will leave the humans alone?"

"He does." I waited for Farley to catch up too. "Who knows, maybe the threat of more humans showing up and waving iron around will be enough to convince them to stay out of the villagers' way. They don't seem to understand people much, but neither does Sylvan. They're a little out of touch with reality."

"Probably on account of how they literally live in another reality," said Farley. "I'd like to stay in this one for the fore-seeable future, thanks."

"Agreed." Out of the corner of my eye, I saw Tam leave the police station and walk the short distance to reach us.

"That's that taken care of," he said. "Are you ready to go?"

"More than ready," said Farley. "There's Maurice."

The vampire had appeared in front of us, as swift and silent as usual. "I'm going to walk back. If those fairies get me lost in the forest again, I won't hesitate to use iron on them."

"Maurice, that's not going to help," said Tam.

"If you run into a certain hunter, though, you're welcome

to make it trickier for him to get home," I added. "If we're leaving him in the forest. Are we?"

"I'll give his team a call when we get back to the tower and tell them to go and get him," said Tam. "I don't think he'll be foolish enough to mess with anyone else. Not after I took his weapons."

"You did?" I asked. "Including the gun? You didn't give it to the police, did you?"

"No." Tam pulled the gun out of his pocket. "Maurice, can I trust you to dispose of this *without* using it on anyone you run into on the way back?"

The vampire worked his jaw. "Except the hunter?"

"Except him." Tam's hand twitched, but he didn't otherwise look affected by handling the gun. How did the iron not harm him? I couldn't ask with the others present, so I waited for him to give the gun to Maurice.

While I might have questioned the wisdom of trusting the vampire with a weapon, Maurice had technically saved my life earlier by dragging me out of the fairy ring. That meant I owed him. *Oh man.*

I'd have to deal with that one later. For now, I lifted my wand, and I transported our group to the gravel path in front of the tower.

The familiar sight brought a rush of relief that vanished in an instant when Tam strode up to the castle's door without meeting my eyes. How could anything go back to normal now? Questions crowded my thoughts, none of which I could voice in front of the others—because I'd given Tam my word, and despite his deception, I didn't intend to break it.

As everyone else went upstairs, I trudged to my own room and changed out of my dirty clothes too. Kellen messaged me twice more while I was in the shower, so once I was dressed, I called him to get it over with.

"Hey." I tried to sound enthusiastic, but my voice came out flat. "I'm back at the tower. We managed to get the children back."

"You did?" Kellen asked. "Did you manage to get them back *without* giving me a ton more paperwork?"

"Well, we don't have a possessed inspector this time, but we do have an unconscious hunter lying in the forest surrounded by fairies who are none too happy with him for stealing their toadstools."

Kellen groaned. "Well. It could be worse. Are you the reason he's unconscious?"

"Not just me. And he deserved it."

"I don't doubt he did," he said. "Go on, tell me everything."

"Honestly, I don't know where to start." The hunter was an obvious place, I supposed. "He's unconscious because he tried to capture an elf who was innocent of any crimes so he could hand him over to the hunters in place of the real kidnappers. Also, it's kind of my fault."

Somehow, I shook the events into order as I began to speak. I had to skip over my argument with Tam and evade explaining how he'd found the way in and out of the fairies' realm without access to glamour, but Kellen didn't ask too many questions.

"And the fairies won't take any more children?" he asked. "I suppose if they did, it'd be out of the Wardens' area unless the people of Pleasance Grove called us again. I did get hold of some of the files, but now the case is over, you won't need them."

"I..." My throat constricted. "Actually, I'd like to read them. There's a lot I don't understand, and it might ... it might help on future cases."

Why was it so hard to speak? Even to Kellen, who I'd never had trouble confiding in before?

"I'll see what I can do, then," he said. "Elves and fairies ...

they're not so different from one another. I'm surprised they don't get along."

"Sylvan is pretty oblivious to the whole situation, to tell you the truth," I said. "I just hope that's enough for the fairies to get the message that he isn't there to threaten them."

"So do I," he said. "Is that all? You have everything you need to write your report?"

"I…" I forced the words out. "Actually, I have something I need to tell you that won't go into the report, but it's not really my secret to tell, and—"

"Perry … the other Wardens already told me," Kellen said. "If you mean the nature of your team leader, that is."

My heart jumped. "Who told you? I didn't think anyone knew…"

"Tam's own supervisor is aware," he said. "The circumstances are difficult, I gather, but he said that he gave Tam the instruction not to tell the rest of his team."

He did? It hadn't just been Tam's own choice? "Why? Why keep a secret like that from us?"

"I imagine for the same reason you try not to tell everyone you meet about your curse."

His words hit me like a blow. "A curse isn't the same as being … being like him. It's not dangerous to others, is it?"

"Actually … in a way, it is," Kellen said. "The fairies, from what I gather, are beings who play by different rules to humans, and Tam had no desire to see his team dragged into their games. That was why he kept it from you."

I thought back to the strange words he and the other fairy had spoken to one another and then to how utterly helpless I'd been when I'd fallen under their spell. Maybe I did get it, a little.

"We did get dragged into it, though." Would there be any turning back now we had? "What should I do?"

"Now?" Kellen asked. "You'll fill out the reports, same as

usual, and we'll hope your next case isn't remotely connected to the fairies."

Our next case. Assuming we had one. "But … I mean, isn't it better to have someone involved who's familiar with the fairies? As opposed to people who have no idea what fairies are capable of?"

"Like I said, it's complicated, and it's not up to me, besides."

"Right." I heard movement outside my room and hoped that nobody had heard every word of our conversation. "I think we should be able to pull the reports together. Erm, can you send those files?"

"If you're sure," he said. "And if you know what you're getting into."

I do … and I don't. "Thanks."

After the call ended, I walked out of my room and almost collided with Tam. "Ah!"

"Sorry I startled you." He took a step back, but at least he met my eyes this time. "I was going to ask who you were talking to."

"Kellen." I hoped he hadn't guessed what files I'd asked for. I didn't know how to explain why I'd asked for them in the first place, when even I wasn't sure of the reasons. Except for having too much curiosity for my own good, that was. "I wanted to wait until we had a decent signal to call him and tell him we'd got the children back."

"Right." A brief silence followed his words, as if he was measuring what to ask next. As if he was as conflicted as me —but not for the same reasons, surely. The ball was in his court now.

Court. Like the fairies…

"I told him about the hunter," I said to avoid prolonging the silence. "In case you hadn't had time to call him yet. And I guess you didn't, because he was talking to me."

He raised a brow. "Did you tell him I knocked Dylan out?"

"No, I skipped over that bit." Not just that bit. The thoughts tangled in my head, strangling the words on the way to my mouth. "I didn't tell him everything. Not … not…"

"That I'm a fairy?"

My chest constricted again when I heard the word he spoke, his tone deceptively casual. "I didn't, but he said your supervisor told him. He also said that…"

"That I was told not to tell my team," he finished. "I always wondered if that would come back to bite me."

"You didn't expect us to never run into any fairies at all?" I kept my voice low in case the others were still in their rooms.

"I did specifically request that we avoid missions with any connection to the fairies, but in this case, we didn't know in advance." He surveyed me, a hint of anxiousness in his features. "And I panicked when I found out. I lost my cool, and I should never have taken it out on you. I'm sorry for that."

The vice grip on my chest tightened. "Why?" I blurted. "Why is it so important that it stays a secret? Do you not trust us?" My voice cracked, treacherously.

His brows shot up "Trust has nothing to do with it," he said. "The fairies are dangerous, and you saw for yourself that they were more than happy to use humans as pawns."

"Yet they're still going to live near the village. Are you sure that'll work out long term?"

"That's for them to decide," he said. "Sylvan seems easygoing for an elf. That should help."

"Why exactly are the elves and fairies at odds?"

"For the same reasons as the feuds between the elves and the covens, and shifters and vampires, and anyone who sees someone else living on their territory as a threat," he replied. "Old rivalries, mistrust, and a lot more. Really, though, the fairies have as many feuds amongst themselves as they do with humans, if not more."

I thought back to the fairy and his words to Tam. "What did he mean by 'divided one'?"

"I'm half-fairy," he said. "Half-human. That was what he meant. Being half-fairy means I'm not immortal like they are. It also means I didn't grow up in their realm. Anyone who's even partially human has a rough time in there."

Oh. That was why he'd been raised by humans. It also meant he wasn't immortal, which... I didn't know why that made me feel as relieved as it did. Maybe it was because it was a sign that he was still Tam. The same person who'd recruited me.

"But you can use ... magic?" I gestured to him. "Glamour?"

"Yes... I use glamour to put on a human face. Almost all half-fairies do, to avoid questions." He glanced down, as if embarrassed. "I grew up with the glamour on. Most of the time I forget I'm wearing it."

I turned his words over in my mind. "So ... you don't mind hiding your real face?"

"Real?" he echoed. "This is my real face, as much as the other. Fairies' relationship with reality is a little complicated."

"Everything to do with the fairies sounds complicated." But I got it, kind of. I wore different faces with different people too. While it stung that he hadn't shared the secret with the rest of us, I knew that he'd thought he was doing the right thing. If Kellen had told me to keep a similar secret when I moved to the tower, I would never have believed it was the wrong decision.

"Yeah." His gaze met mine. "I didn't realise that you'd see it as a deception, which was foolish of me. I don't blame you for being angry with me."

I shook my head. "No, I—I don't see it that way. Back then I was freaked out, yes, but that was because we were in a world where everything wanted to kill us."

What am I saying? Yes, he'd deceived me, but that was nothing on the misery I'd felt when he'd wanted me gone. When I'd turned up to help him and he'd acted as if I'd been the betrayer.

His expression relaxed minutely. "Yes, there is that. I did wonder if I'd face judgment, but in a way, it's … it's a relief that someone knows. Someone other than my supervisor."

"What?" My voice squeaked out, and I cringed inwardly. "I thought you didn't want me to know. I got the impression it was the worst thing that ever happened to you when I followed you to Sylvan's house."

"No." Shock flitted across his face. "No. That wasn't what I meant at all. Like I said, I panicked, and I made the wrong call when I left you all behind without explaining anything either. I just didn't know how much to tell you without giving it away, and I was worried about drawing the fairies' attention towards you too."

"Of course." I inhaled. "I'm sorry I barged in where I wasn't wanted. I shouldn't have assumed you didn't have it handled alone."

"I should have communicated better," he said. "It wasn't that you weren't wanted. I was scared for you and the team, and I should never have yelled at you like that."

Heat rushed up my neck. I didn't know what to say, but relief that he wasn't angry with me overtook all other thoughts. "I was scared too. I thought you were dead, or … or gone."

Damn. I didn't mean to sound as needy as I did, and I hoped he didn't pick up any vibes other than those of a concerned teammate. It didn't help that I suspected my face had gone as red as one of those toadstools.

"I won't let it happen again," he said. "My secret isn't more important than the team's safety."

"I didn't…" I swallowed. "Then you don't think I'm a nuisance who can't follow orders and screws everything up?"

"What?" He shook his head. "Absolutely not. You might be a little rash sometimes, but you saved my neck back there. If you hadn't been there, the hunter would have put a bullet in me."

The heat in my face became an inferno. "No … no, Maurice was there too. I was just…"

"Don't dismiss yourself like that," he said. "You followed me when nobody else did. Why would I condemn you for that?"

"Oh." As he kept watching me, my insides stirred with feelings that were entirely unsuitable to a heart-to-heart between a team leader and one of his colleagues. "Good."

"I hope that clears it up," he said. "I understand why you wanted to tell Kellen, but the others…"

"You want to tell them yourself, I know." I broke my gaze from his, the heat fading as a familiar sadness arose inside me. "I get it. I know what it's like. Keeping a secret from people for their own sakes."

The curse wasn't the same as his secret, I knew, but the end result was the same. When the truth came out, people got hurt.

"The curse." A pause followed. "It's okay if you don't want to tell me, but what did the Seer actually see when she first looked at you?" he asked.

"I have no idea," I said. "None of them do either. It's just scary enough to drive them into a screaming fit. Trust me, having a pair of hidden wings is nothing by comparison."

He frowned, as if my flippant tone didn't entirely fool him. "Fairies don't show up in visions, like vampires. That was why she had so much trouble pinning them down … and it was likely why she didn't see our team inside the crystal ball either."

"Poor Mrs Hutchins." I was seized with the bizarre urge to laugh at the absurdity of it all. "When she contacted the Wardens, she didn't bargain on ending up with a cursed witch, a fairy, and a vampire, did she?"

"I guess not," he said. "Though I wondered ... could a Seer figure out the nature of your curse?"

"Why would they want to?" I asked. "Even if they weren't scared out of their mind by the sight of me, there's no way to undo the curse. Short of the person who cast it on me dropping dead."

His frown deepened, and I sensed the need to change the subject. "Anyway, I did have a couple of questions for you about being a fairy."

"Oh?" Wariness filled his voice. "Such as..."

"Your abilities," I said. "You can fly, move faster than humans ... oh, and you can't have your mind read by a vampire. Anything else?"

"Those are all the advantages," he answered. "I'm also unable to handle cold iron without side effects."

"Like pure iron? What happens?"

"Uncontrollable sneezing, mostly."

I stared at him. Then I burst out laughing. "Seriously?"

"Yes." He angled himself towards the stairs. "I also have sharp hearing, almost as sharp as a shifter's, which is how I know the others are getting impatient with us."

Sure enough, Maurice's voice drifted up from below. "Are you two ever going to come downstairs?"

"In a minute," Tam called back. "Is that all right, Perry?"

He wasn't just asking that. He wanted to know if I was all right with everything—with keeping his secret, with staying on the team, with fighting side by side.

I was. Without question. "Yeah. We'll be right there."

ABOUT THE AUTHOR

Elle Adams lives in the middle of England, where she spends most of her time reading an ever-growing mountain of books, planning her next adventure, or writing. Elle's books are humorous mysteries with a paranormal twist, packed with magical mayhem.

She also writes urban and contemporary fantasy novels as Emma L. Adams.

Visit http://www.elleadamsauthor.com/ to find out more about Elle's books.